Queen Shulamith's Ball

Mary Catelli

Published by Wizard's Wood Press, 2019.

QUEEN SHULAMITH'S BALL

First edition. October 16, 2019.

Copyright © 2019 Mary Catelli.

ISBN: 978-1-942564-64-5

Written by Mary Catelli.

Queen Shulamith's Ball

A ball, a ball, Queen Shulamith would hold a ball. . . .

Throughout the city, down every street, sibilant rumors ran. Even the birds, drab or jewel-bright, twittered of the rumors in their nests, tucked in the crevices of gray stone carvings. On a street corner, a drunkard, in tatters of green and scarlet, waved his bottle in air and—with marginal coherence—declaimed on how the ball would change the lives of many within the city before he slumped against the lamppost, and then to the pavement, to snore. And every passerby, eyeing the gray stone of the houses on her street, was sure to pick out hers.

When, in the gray early morning, Queen Shulamith appeared on her front steps, between the pillars, her violet gown swept the stone. She wore no jewelry, but her black hair, braided, wound about her head like a crown. The crowd shifted as people glanced and murmured. A sour old peddler, unable to hawk his apples when no one looked at him, muttered that it wasn't as if the city didn't have a ball, or two or three, every week. The queen paid none of them the least heed as she spoke with servants.

Two little girls walked in their white pinafores and blue dresses—black-haired Carol and little fair-haired Nina—to Queen Hesione's refined school, founded after her husband drank the money from selling their crowns. They passed the peddler without buying an apple and whispered of Queen Shulamith. She was only a queen, after all, like Queen Hesione, or the aunt of one girl and the second cousin of the other. She had to be an exile, too, or she would be making treaties and negotiating alliances. For all her grand house, if she lost her money, Queen Shulamith might open a school, too. . . .

Holding hands, they ran up the stairs.

"Are you?" piped Nina, quieting the square. "Are you really holding a ball?"

Queen Shulamith smiled down at the girls. "Yes." Her voice carried over the square in a sudden stillness. "Young people must meet, after all. Young or old, we must amuse ourselves, and tongues and hearts of flint must find some way to gather as well, or they will risk their health, wading through poor weather to gossip, and then they would die in their sins."

Baffled, but remembering their etiquette classes, the girls thanked her. They forgot everything else as they scrambled down the steps, but they assured everyone they met that Queen Shulamith would give a ball, until they climbed the stairs to the school and did not quite tell all the other girls before Queen Hesione hushed them and sent them to their classes. One little girl, in the corridors, said, scornfully, that they would have been wiser to ask about the queen's magical mirrors, everyone knew Queen Shulamith had magical mirrors in her house like nothing else in the city, and balls were every day. The other girls resolved to listen at the windows.

Even with the windows open, little drifted in, as people talked of this and that, about the river ribbons and the scandal about Lady Rose-Lily, and only now and again about Queen Shulamith—and Queen Hesione or another teacher called them back to dreariness of history or mathematics or embroidery, while every other tongue in the square carried the tale further, and the news passed on from mouth to mouth, engulfing the city like a tide. Girls just old enough to attend exulted in their age, and lorded over their younger sisters, who pouted that a few years—or months, or weeks—cut them off from such a marvel, when Queen Shulamith never held balls. Maidens old enough to be sure murmured about the promise, and peril, of her famed magical mirrors, and whether it was wise to attend a ball where unknown magic could affect them all. Shopkeepers, whether selling lace or cloth or feathers, or any frippery at all, calculated their prices and how much more they could sell for such a novelty; the fancy, attending the ball, would not let themselves wear only such finery as would do for a more common ball, given by a more ordinary queen. Hostesses made haughty, cutting re-marks about how she had obviously chosen the time to undercut their own balls.

Out on a street corner, a dark-haired young woman in a flame-col-ored gown danced with a bear. A scattering of coins fell. After each dance, she gathered coins and turned to dance again, except when she and the bear moved to a new corner. In her pirouettes, Gemma half-heard the whispers about where she came from, and those of other things. Queen Shulamith's ball caught her ear, as much as she dared lis-ten. One girl, pouting, told her mother she would never get to attend so fine a ball, and Gemma pirouetted outward, into her path.

"I might be at the ball, to dance and amuse the guests—" Her voice rang over the cobblestones. "—but you can watch me dancing here be-fore then."

The mother hustled the girl onward. Gemma, a half-smile on her lips, turned back to dancing with the bear. A delivery boy shook his head and went on. At the Golden Bird bakery, he joined with a cooking girl to ape those fancy dancers in pirouettes that sent flour flying. Laughter and applause engulfed them, until the baker shouted them back to work. The delivery boy took the next batch and fled out the door, down a street full of stalls.

An old man, smoking his pipe before his stall of pots, watched the boy run. He would not speak first of the ball himself, but whenever a customer, or a passerby, spoke of it, he took out the pipe to pronounce that this ball would produce many a change in the city, mark his words and watch them happen.

Even on High Street, where all the narrow but high houses rose ten and twelve floors, in a parlor on a seventh floor, when they gathered in the morning (just before noon), the gossiping women mentioned the ball before Alixandre said that a knight's wife had given birth to a fox. "Or so it was said."

"Really," said Blanca, lifting her tea cup, "the lower orders are getting entirely above themselves."

"I blame Queen Lenore," said Ida. "She gave them all the idea—giving birth to a bear prince!" She waved her hand over the tea set, with its painted pink rosebuds and its inlay of gold. "And then everyone from the duchesses down to the wives of knights took it up."

"Let us just hope that it doesn't get down into the commoners." Alixandre went to pour herself another cup of tea. "Who knows what they would do? Cats from a merchant's wife?"

"Worse," said Blanca, "it might get out to the peasants, and we will hear of rabbit children."

Alixandre's mouth twisted. "I suppose we will have to wait and see about that—one never can tell—why, I even heard that there is to be another invasion of the city!"

"Really?" said Ida.

"Really," said Alixandre. "One would think they never learned."

"Some people do," said Blanca. "They come to the city nonetheless, for all the rumors." She pointed out the window. For the first time since they gathered, the other women looked out. It took some effort, with the parlor's height, and the morning leaving the street engulfed in shadow, but still they could see the carriage down on the ribbon of a street.

Ida eyed the sky and sipped some tea. "Early to arrive. One wonders when they left, and where they spent the night."

Beneath her eye, the carriage trundled along the street, through towering houses, with their white-washed, half-timbered stories—and down and down, past the heights of High Street, and then along River Street, with its heavy stone walls and piers. Where the blocks of stone stood taller than most men. Where the stone descended in a stairway down to the waters with their rushes. On the walls, a handful of maidens, as green and brown as the rushes, perched and made ribbons.

The youngest looked brightly up at the carriage. "Another one! We will—this ball of Queen Shulamith's will do us so much good. So many ribbons and trinkets for it—"

The other women laughed like rippling water. One said, "A ribbon not made never sells, however grand a ball is held."

The youngest looked obediently back to her ribbon, so that Marjorie, looking out the carriage window, saw only bowed heads and neat brown hair. She folded her hands in her lap. The carriage trundled on through a drab and crowded city. It did not look as if it could possibly be a suitable place to bring out a young woman, let alone the only possible one.

The road rose again, though not as much as High Street had risen. Her aunt lived on the river's other bank. Marjorie looked at the masses of buildings where the bank rose, and hoped that the description did not merely indicate which half of the city the house stood in.

She let her breath out. Perhaps the city was more pleasant than it looked, with its narrow streets and endless gray houses. She knew her mother, and her aunt, would never let her leave here again without settling her. If she died an old maid, she would die here. For a minute, her eyes stared out the window without seeing anything. Six months ago, it had all been arranged that she would come with her cousin, and her cousin's husband and their two little boys. Merely because the cousin and husband had died, her mother had thought, was no reason for her not to come out now. She shivered. She had not seen her cousin Artemise in seven years; she had never even met her sons. Perhaps she never would meet the boys, now.

The carriage lurched to a stop and made her blink. Her elderly companion snorted and pulled her black shawl closer.

"Ridiculous, the way people do not—just because the city is rife with exiles, they do not know how to treat gentry— even an exiled king should not be treated like a beggar—a mere entertainer, blocking *our* way!"

Marjorie leaned half out the window. In a square ahead of them, music played—magically, she could see no musicians—and a brown bear danced, hand in paw, with a dark-haired woman in a flame-red gown that flared like a poppy. The woman herself, and the bear, did not stand in the way, but a crowd clumped around—fishwives, peddlers, servants with packages. After all, this was the morning. Even if the gentry, or nobility, or royalty, had risen, they would not be about, to watch. Marjorie let out her breath. Well, except fools like herself, who might be about, for all their higher birth. She did not sit back.

The bear pirouetted, and Marjorie eyed it. She had seen dancing bears before, and poor pitiful things they had been. This bear, with its shaggy brown coat, could *dance*.

The bear's claws, gleaming like ivory, passed very close to the woman, and Marjorie shivered. The woman curtsied the bear bowed, the music ended, and the crowd, with a shower of coins before the dancers, shuddered, and broke up, laughing and chattering. A girl's voice wondered if the bear would come to Queen Shulamith's ball, and Marjorie, sitting back, wondered how long it would take for her to learn that tale.

"Finally!" The companion eyed Marjorie, who looked back at her hands.

The carriage turned a corner. An empty street spread before them.

"At least here they have proper back streets," grumbled the duenna. "Where the riffraff can come to the back door."

The carriage rumbled up before a house looking like many another on this street, and in other streets: square, solid, built of gray stone, four stories with glass windows looking out. Wrought iron, in filigrees more sinuous than vines, stood before the windows.

As her luggage came down, Marjorie stood in the street and tightened her hands on the fabric of her skirt. The day before she would have thought the house tall. Now, after the towering concoctions on High

Street, she could barely keep from thinking them short. But still, she did not like the sight of them.

A window opened. A young woman, still dressed in a morning wrap, her hair a mass of pale brown curls, looked over the ironwork. Marjorie tried to remember who she was, and what her name was, but before she could, the other woman turned back to call, without much enthusiasm, into the house.

"Aunt Maude! She made it! She's here, she's arrived!"

Moments later, the door opened, and Maude, muttering about "this early," swept out with servants to take the luggage. While they hustled it within, she exchanged greetings and farewells with the duenna, and ushered Marjorie inside, to a hall of white-washed walls, with a mirror by the door, ready for a departing woman to give her beauty one last inspection.

The other young woman had come down the stairs. She stood on the last of the dark wood steps and looked vaguely discontented.

"Henrietta," said Maud, "this is Marjorie my niece." She waved at Henrietta. "My goddaughter, come here for the festivities as you have."

Marjorie looked down, at the dark wood of the floor. And for the young men, no doubt.

Maude closed the door and looked her up and down. "Though I dare say her mother readied her better than you. Your hair!"

The journey had not left her hair in wild disarray; she could barely eye it, even out of the corner of her eye. In the mirror, she saw nothing conspicuous about it: pale blond, pretty, perhaps her best feature.

"Whatever did your mother think, letting you dye it? *Quite* out of fashion. Everyone knows that women dye their hair to try to pass themselves off as fairer than they are. Waste of money, she clearly spent a pretty penny to get it that shade. It looks natural."

As if it were not her own, her hand moved up, as stiffly as the arm of a watermill, to pull forward a lock of her hair. It looked as it always had.

"It's blond by nature," said Marjorie, barely audibly.

She had spoken loudly enough to be heard; Maud eyed her and then shrugged.

"We shall just dye it, then. Black, I think. Suits you better than brown. And your eyebrows as well. A good thing we have spells to do the thing properly."

Marjorie stood like stone. And to think her parents had sent her to Maud only because her mother had not wanted to change the timing. Artemise would not have dyed her hair black, even if only because her hair was blond.

Maud bustled her up the stairs. "A pity you will not be ready for King Magnus's fete, but you can't be."

"I can be," said Henrietta. "I've sewed everything. I've spent hours. . .."

"Most improper," said Maude, climbing onward, not glancing at her. "I must get Marjorie ready. If her mother did not have her hair dyed, she must have failed in many things. And you can not go alone."

Henrietta grimaced and still followed them up the stairs, but when Maude bustled Marjorie into a backroom, overlooking the garden, Henrietta continued to walk along the hallway. Marjorie glanced about the room, with its pale yellow wallpaper and the furnishings, and the window overlooking the garden. She got barely a glimpse of the blossoming roses, and the promised back street behind it, before Maude turned on her.

"You do know to hold your tongue about Konigsburg?"

Marjorie nodded. "Konigsburg, and Kingsbury, and any other name. I will speak of the city, and use no other name, which will cause no offense among those from other kingdoms and lands."

"Not just among the fancy," said Maude. "Even the servant and shopkeepers—" She glanced out the doorway and realized her other charge had walked rather slower than she should have. Trying to eavesdrop, no doubt.

"Henrietta, I've told you to avoid pouting like that. You will do it in public and offend people—besides, it is not becoming."

Henrietta grimaced and stalked onward. She had paid attention only long enough to find something to embarrass her. Now, Maude would fuss over Marjorie and pay *her* no more attention than she paid the kitchen cat. No, less—she would curse the cat if it caught no mice. When Marjorie—if she were not silly—would *want* her to go to the fetes and balls. Then she would be introduced, and could introduce Marjorie to all the people when she went. Marjorie would have to like that better than sitting in the corner.

It would even help her be ready for Queen Shulamith's ball.

Henrietta reached her room, where the window overlooked the street, and glowered at the wallpaper. Not that Maude's fussing would prove much help to Marjorie. Already *she* had stayed here three months, and Lady Maude's vaunted sponsorship had not won her so much as a man expressing a wish to know her better. And she had worked so hard to be ready for King Magnus's ball.

She went over to the window. The street did not bustle, but was not utterly empty; a carriage rattled along, like the one that had brought Marjorie. She turned away; it would not be someone calling, not at this hours, and indeed, the carriage rattled on, down the street, about the corner, and up a hillside.

Inside sat two pale-haired little boys, their faces salt white and all the paler by their charcoal gray clothes, their jerkins laced up with dark blue ribbons.

The younger stirred, looked out the window, and said, without much spirit, "Is that the house?"

Michel shook his head, without looking up. Even out of the corner of his eye, he had seen the stone fronting the street. Most of the grown-ups had talked over his head, but he had heard *some* things.

"Not yet, Philippe."

Philippe sank back down, as subdued as Michel. The coach trundled on, turned a corner, and stopped. Michel slowly looked up. A great, pale house stood before them. Between them and it, a wall of white stone held up wrought iron railings, and between that wall and the house, statues stood: a slender young angel, her hands on high, her face imploring; a dragon, every scale distinct, coiled and ready to burn some soul alive; a monkey-like imp posed in some caper; and more. Three gray-barked trees stood among them, their very trunks bent.

The house itself bore more statuary, carved little winged children, and curlicues and festoons about arched windows. It had room enough to hold them both, and half a hundred other children at need; the house stood larger than a king's castle.

"Ho, young masters, we haven't got all day," snarled the coachman, as he climbed down from his seat. "Don't sit like lumps." He hauled open the door, and Michel stumbled out, feeling wobbly, as if the earth lurched the way the carriage had.

"Ho, now," said the coachman. Michel turned. Philippe stood in the carriage's door, blinking. The coachman scooped him down to the ground, none too gently, and said, "To the door, to the door, you think we've got all day?"

"Will the sun set early?" said Philippe, timidly, and the coachman raised his hand, as if to knock him over. Philippe stepped closer to Michel, who took his hand and rushed off with him, toward the house. They hurried along the white flagstones of the path with the coachman stalking after them, through the none-too-green garden, where red mushrooms grew.

Over the steps to the doorway, a snow leopard slumped. Its tufted ears twitched a little in its slumbers, its head rested on its forepaws, and its long sleek body spread as if to annex as much of the stairs as it could. Its pale gray spots flexed as it breathed. Philippe grabbed onto Michel's arm with both hands. Michel tried not to stare. He had to be brave, he couldn't frighten Philippe. . . but they had to live here, in this house, with that creature that slept on the doorstep.

The coachman gawked at it. Then, with a shudder, he reached for the knocker, a fantastic contraption like a knotted ribbon made of lead. It clomped against the door solidly; the noise sounded, but did not echo.

And it did not rouse the snow leopard. It slumbered on, its flanks rising and falling as it breathed.

Clinging to his brother's hand, Michel looked over the garden. Some grass did grow there, though low against the ground. One tree stood bent like the crescent moon, and for a moment, he thought he saw a face in the bark.

The door opened, slowly but silently. From behind it, without moving out of the hall's shadows, an old, old man looked out. He still stood straight, but his white hair foamed about his head and into a beard, and his face bore more wrinkles than a withered old apple. His narrowed eyes looked down at them.

"So these are my great-great-grandsons," he said, his voice scratchy.

The coachman bowed and retreated in silence. Philippe stepped closer to Michel, and Michel's grip tightened.

Their great-great-grandfather sniffed. "The door's open. What fanciness do you need to come in?"

Philippe's hand tightened until he felt like an anchor, but the coach already rattled along the street without them. Michel swallowed. The city had other coaches. Not one would take two orphaned boys with nowhere to go and no coin to pay. He inched inside, and Philippe clung to him, so close that they nearly tripped over each other's feet.

Without so much as stepping back in order to give them a place to stand, their great-great-grandfather peered down at them. His eyes narrowed more—Michel had not realized that was possible—and he sniffed again.

"*What* were they thinking? Your clothing is *far* too merry for children in morning. Such festive ribbons! Blue! When your parents have died!"

Michel looked down at them.

"You will go to the tailor for new clothing." He turned from the door. A desk stood by it, of dark red wood, so tall than even a grown man like their great-great-grandfather had to stand to write at it. His pen scratched, and a minute later, he stamped the letter with red sealing wax, and handed it to Michel. Michel took the letter but stared at it. It could have been a curse that would turn them both into statues, for all he could see. The grotesque gargoyle on the seal grinned back at him.

Philippe pulled closer to him.

"I trust you can recognize a tailor's shop?" said their great-great-grandfather, coldly.

He had seen enough shop signs to know a tailor's. Michel nodded.

"Turn left when you reach the street. Old Wat knows better than to cheat me." He loomed over them. Michel stepped back, out of the doorway again. Philippe stumbled out with him. "The first tailor on the street."

The door shut. The snow leopard yawned, a great gap of scarlet opening in its face. Michel swallowed. It eyed them lazily, as if considering whether two such small mouthfuls were worth the effort of getting up. After a moment, it settled again, its head lazing on its paws, not a hint of red showing.

"Come, Philippe," said Michel, his voice wobbling.

They inched outward, and looked from side to side in the garden, seeing, now, statues like butterflies, and others like snails. But even walking slowly, they reached the street, and Michel walked along it, holding Philippe's hand. As far as he could see down the way, there were no shops at all, not a single sign hanging over the street, or even a building that fronted the street. They plodded on, in front of great houses like their great-great-grandfather's, with their walled gardens, and their pale stone, until his legs ached from the distance.

One house, built of icy white stone, bustled with life as servants arrayed it with flowers, in pots and in garlands, in pinks and reds, and greenery, to conceal the stone. Others put in place statues, to stand on pedestals and walls, and in nooks in the walls, but not statues of the pale stone like their great-great-grandfather's garden. These were metallic and enameled in a glorious array of colors: birds and harlequins, jugglers with their balls, dancers arrayed for a dazzling ball, and many of those with crowns. Phillipe's eyes were round, and he turned his head to watch the servants' work, until he stumbled because he looked behind them. Michel pulled him on, and they looked down the street of pale houses, unadorned.

Behind them, with much profanity and shouted orders, the servants went on with the array, ignoring any passers-by.

"They had best think all this greenery is something fine," grumbled one. "It's worse than statues, with all the prickles."

"As long as they pay for the work, it hardly matters," said another. He shifted the rose garland in his hand, and cursed, looking at the blood a thorn had drawn from his finger, and turned his attention back to the garlands. No time to even notice passers-by. They had to put out the lights as well.

The day inched onward. Servants climbed on ladders to bedeck the niches on the fourth and fifth floors, with blossoms and candles, and the air grew scented with the blooms. At nightfall, with the last leaves and flowers barely in place, flame leapt magically up in lamps and candles, to shine on the guests who swept in. Girls, new to the city, or so young they had not attended such galas before, gawked and had to be hustled onward before they were laughed at as green. Two girls squealed as the older girl pointed out a figure with a red beard and red hair, wearing a golden crown and a suit of metallic peacock green—"Like King Magnus himself!" said the younger.

"Hush," said her mother. "You can not squeal so at a mere party and expect me to take you to Queen Shulamith's ball."

The girl pouted. "You take me to balls, I can go to balls."

"As long as you are well," said her mother. "Girls who can go to balls can still suffer from such *fearful* headaches that they can not go anywhere at all. Queen Shulamith will accept such an excuse and be full of sympathy." She swept up the stairs, her subdued daughters following.

By the doorway, a lean, tall man with gray in his black hair bowed to her. He wore black, that invariable refuge of the poor—feigned mourning to avoid the cost of finer clothing, indifferent to the crow-like air they brought to festivities—and his black was shabbier than most even of them.

He spoke politely enough, bowing and saying, "You were fortunate, my lady. You came just in time for the last dance."

The mother frowned. The ball would last all hours. To end before midnight was a shame, and many lasted until dawn.

"Gemma will leave after this."

She scowled. Such an entertainment, at a ball—and her girls looked delighted.

"The last—" the older one whispered, and they pressed forward, past their mother. The center of the room held a bear. With it stood a woman in a flame-red gown, her black hair floating over her shoulders like a cloak.

Their mother sniffed. "For King Magnus to bring such a creature here, and his keeper is hardly better—we could see this any day on the street."

"And suffer the crowds' impertinence?" said the man.

The music struck up, and her daughters did not stay for the conversation but pressed into the room. The bear held out its paw, the woman took it, and they footed it through a stately measure. The mother muttered that her own daughters should be ashamed, not enraptured, as they did not dance as well as the beast, and others about the hall murmured of the skill as well.

"No common bear, this one," called one young man as Gemma curtsied, and the bear bowed. Gemma's face did not move; it felt like a mask. She still wondered how she did it. It felt strange, as she straightened, not to hear the patter of coins at her feet yet. She knew that their fee would exceed the take on the street, but—how swiftly she had grown accustomed to being a mountebank!

"The bear prince," called a young woman. When every eye turned on her, she blanched and said, more hesitantly, "The—Queen Lenore's third child. She would have taught him to dance, with the rest of a prince's education. . . ." It did not slackening the staring, and her words faltered into silence.

Gemma put her hands on her hips. Her jaw tightened. "The bear prince? Queen Lenore's son? But everyone knows that the bear prince lives with the queen his mother in the forest, in *seclusion*." She waved one hand, sweeping the entire hall and all the guests. "Clearly, then, since he is the bear prince, you are all enchantments that the court magicians conjured to amuse both mother and son. Perhaps you are all really *trees*, and can only move and dance for his delight." She drew the hand back against herself, framing her throat. Mountebank. She had to convince them of that. "Therefore it behooves you all to be generous to us. Your money must be as enchanted and unreal as you yourselves are—stinting will not benefit you—it will dissolve into leaves for you as well as it will for me."

Laughter resounded, and the clink of money on stone. Candlelight glinted from the metal, and Gemma went to gathered up coins with the eagerness they would expect from some poor peasant lass. The bear snuffled at the coins, drawing laughter, and then the crowd eased off, toward some other room, some other amusement, chattering about this ball and that, and whether Queen Shulamith would send them all invitations, and whether the ball could truly match the wonders they saw every month, surely a monarch accustomed to giving balls would do better than one who never did, and whether that would stop anyone from attending.

Gemma did not care, as long as they left; their invitations would not determine hers. As the guests thinned, King Magnus's servants came toward her, picking the coins up. They pocketed at least half of them, she knew, but she eyed them, the bear beside her, and they yielded some.

The bear snorted. Gemma turned. On all fours, its black nose snuffling at the air, the bear leaned toward a whip-lean man, brown in coloring and clothing. Even on all fours, its height came nearly to the man's shoulder. It eyed his hands, and its fangs showed bare and sharp.

"He is *helping* us," scolded Gemma. "Helping gather our coins. You should not be so mistrustful. I am sure he will not steal them." She smiled at the servant. Then she approached and held out her hand. That servant handed over twice as many coins as all his fellows.

Gemma, her mouth twisting, held them out for a moment before pocketing them. "See?"

The bear gave a sound, half snort, half growl, and its paw pushed a coin over the floor. Gemma dropped to one knee to add it to their hoard. Better than the streets, she noted, even without the fee.

Then, thanking the servants but offering not a penny, she went for her cloak, to muffle herself in its dark folds, and she and the bear headed outside and crossed the chessboard of bright and dark where the windows shone down.

King Magnus's house and its light fell behind, and no one else nearby gave a fete on this night; dark, moonless night folded round them. Only a ribbon of stars, directly overhead, was not hidden by the buildings to either side. Gemma shivered. Though the city seemed less oppressive by day than when they had first arrived, she had not gotten used to its night.

"We have no need of the money," said the bear, its voice deep and growling.

"We do," said Gemma, without a glance aside. "We need money enough so that no one will question whether we earned what we spend, or whether we came to the city to earn money."

To that charge, the bear offered no counter-argument. They ambled down the street until Gemma could smell the water of the river as the bear could. There, they headed down a side alleyway to a stable. The horses had all been removed, and the stable cleaned, for the gold Gemma could pay.

She closed the door carefully behind them, shutting them into the dark and the smell of straw, and ensuring no outside light seeped in, before she began her conjuration. It took a minute, with the straw rustling into new shapes, but then they stood in a room with a lit lamp, a heap of rugs to make the bear a bed, and an actual bed for her.

"Easier by daylight." The bear sat on its haunches. "When you don't have to be so careful about the light."

"I'd have timed it closer if I had known that mattered," said Gemma. "It's not as if I brought us back early because I hoped to go to the library."

The bear grunted. Gemma went to the door to look out.

"Don't you?" said the bear. "Hope?"

"Hope, yes," said Gemma. The street outside was empty. "Brought, you may have noticed, no." She stepped into the doorway. "I'm going down to the river, for a breath of air."

She closed the door behind her, quickly. In the cool and the dark, she let her breath out. The bear would go to bed, and she would have to find her way in, in the dark. But she did not think she could have stayed there much longer. He treated her like a servant—

She *was* a servant, Gemma told herself. The night breeze, cooling, tugged at her skirts. Queen Lenore meant well, raising the poor orphan herself, but she should have had her fostered by a suitable family of wizards. She eased her way down the alley. She was not even noble. Yes, her father had been a wizard in Queen Lenore's service, and he had died saving the queen, but a just reward for that was to raise the little orphan and give her her father's place, which Queen Lenore had done. Sending her as a servant with the prince showed how highly the queen trusted her.

When she reached the street, a carriage creaked down it, with four lanterns marking it out. Gemma turned, to walk toward the river. From the clock tower, the clock face gleamed like a moon, but Gemma did not even glance at it, as the hour hardly mattered. The air smelled of water and rushes. Light glowed among the rushes, and Gemma's mouth twisted. The women there no doubt conjured homes out of mud, as she did from straw, and wove their ribbons from flowers. Or rushes, and then used magical dyes.

Under the bridge itself, fires burned, surrounded by the other entertainers of the street. They wore a mix and match of the brilliance of their costumes and drab, sensible travel wear. The fire gilded parts of the scene and cast enormous shadows over the rest.

A boy plucked at a lute, a tune drifting over the waters. A dark young woman—Gemma had seen her dancing, and hailed as "the elegant Esmeralda"—shook out her green skirt, and her gaze fell across Gemma.

"Ho, fellows," Esmeralda called, her voice ringing. "Watch what secrets we tell." She shook the skirt harder. "We have a *rival* watching us."

Gemma stopped. All the eyes had turned on her, firelight glinting from eyeballs and casting shadows over their faces. After a minute, when none of them turned away, she said, thinly, "You have new dances for my bear?"

Laughter echoed raucously from stone and waters. Gemma drew back, along the bank. The city's enchantments made its streets safer than most, but she did not quite turn her back on them until the firelight vanished behind her, and there was the clock's light—as bright as a half moon, at least.

Another light gleamed across the river: bobbing along. A candleman, thought Gemma. A plump man wrapped in ramshackle coats of bright reds and purples, with his candles arrayed about the brim of his hat—he ambled along with their usual leisure. Two little charges, fair-haired and dressed in black, scurried alongside, or fell back and hurried to join up again, because slow though his pace was, he did not slow further when the boys were not by him. She scowled, but—what could she do? Being scolded by a woman who danced on the street with a bear would hardly frighten a candleman, especially without the bear.

He proceeded down the street, out of her sight, and the boys ran after. A moon-pale owl flitted, silently, after them. In the moments when it caught such light as there was, no one saw it, and moments later it veered off into an alleyway. The candleman trudged on.

Philippe, catching up, looked warily up at him. Michel kept his gaze to the street, but the candleman, with his bleary eyes and bloodshot face, frightened Philippe. Even that great, broad-brimmed hat with a row of candles around the edge: they shed light, but he did not like it.

"What's that?" said Michel, pointing to the light across the river. Philippe peered, following his finger to under the bridge: a reddish glow, like a fire.

"Eh," said the candleman, without looking aside, "who knows? Nobody who matters, down by the river. Even by day, only time the fancy go down is to buy ribbons." He turned, and they crossed a bridge to the other side, and up the street. Michel yawned, and felt no more curiosity about the light. He peered ahead hoping for his great-great-grandfather's house before he fell asleep in the street.

Something—something small—floated through the air ahead.

The candleman said, sullenly, "Eh, do not like this Winter Street. Tailor shoulda paid more. I'd've made him, knew it was Winter Street."

Michel scowled at the little flecks. Were they really—then he put out his tongue and caught one snowflake on it. It melted. He looked at Philippe, who looked back with enormous eyes.

But as they walked on, the boys stumbling from exhaustion, snow sifted over the street, and the stones grew slick. Philippe slipped on one rounded one, and Michel ran to help him. His legs hurt, they had walked for so long, and stood for so long to be fitted.

"Come along, boys, come along," said the candleman, not breaking his stride, his voice containing no encouragement. "In the snow, it's not wise to linger on the street."

Michel glared at him, and the boys scrambled to keep up, stifling their yawns.

Their great-great-grandfather's house finally stood ahead. The candlelight shot enormous shadows up against the walls and in the hollows of the sculptures, distorting the statuary into unrecognizable forms, with mouths and claws that seemed ready to snatch.

Michel and Philippe clung to each other's hands, peering about, as they walked toward the door, and Michel tripped over the candleman's heels. He did not even glance back. Michel peered around him to see the snow leopard still asleep on the doorway. Snow had drifted up beside it.

"Ho, now, I delivered you home, that was my instruction, and so I bid you good day." The candleman walked off, more briskly than he had walked with them. The candle flames swirled with his passage, sending the shadows whirling, shrinking, swelling, and Michel scrambled past the leopard to knock on the door.

The knocker was loud, left no echo, and stirred no response. For all Michel could tell, as the sound faded, the house had long been abandoned and hollow, with no one having set foot in it for many a day, or year. Even the leopard was not roused. He bit his lip and tried the door. It opened, still silently. Though the air was warmer, the light was even less inside than out. Splotches of moonlight, through the windows, lay along the hallway like the pale spots of a dark leopard.

The leopard yawned and shifted.

The boys scrambled inside, and Michel shut the door as swiftly as it would move. It closed with a clunk heavier than the knocker's, stirring neither echo nor any movement.

They stood for a minute. The air was still, and a trifle warmer than outside. Moonlight filtered through enormous windows, showing long whitewashed halls, with winding staircases built of dark wood, and doors of the same wood.

Michel let his breath out. "Let's go to bed," he said, trying to sound brave, and the words echoed a little.

"How?" said Philippe. "*He* didn't say where to sleep. Didn't—" He yawned. "—see anywhere instead."

"Some rooms here have to have beds," said Michel.

Philippe eyed the stairs. "What if—" His voice grew smaller, more ghost-like. "What if we find *his* bedroom?"

Michel swallowed. "Then we'll ask him where to sleep," he said, though his voice trembled.

They climbed to the next floor, with moonlight falling on their steps now and again. There, they tried door after door, each of which opened silently on rooms lined with books, or set with tables and chairs, or even nothing at all, only a bare four walls and windows. If they had found only one with a couch, he would have dared it, but they did not.

They did not speak loudly, but their voices echoed despite themselves, and when they had passed, the dark wood seemed darker, and the pale walls paler. Finally, they found a small, whitewashed room with a lead-paned window and two small beds. A servant's room, thought Michel, but there, they crawled in, to sleep within moments. The house lowered with disapproval about them. Even the owls, bats, and pale moths gave it a wide berth by moonlight, and none of the morning's birdsong came from its trees.

The house still lowered on, even as the next day grew bright and cloudless. The passersby, afoot or in carriage, tended to hurry by it. When Maude's carriage trundled by, Marjorie eyed it. Even among the great mansions. . . .

"That's an unpleasant place," she said.

Maude shrugged. Marjorie turned to face her. Her own hair shifted in the movement, and she winced. She wondered when the sight would no longer startle her, those raven tresses instead of her own honey blond, but Maude had set to at once, to leave nothing to chance.

"It's not like the old man living there cares much," said Henrietta, oblivious to her thoughts, not even looking out the window. "I mean, his *great-grandson* just died. Old man, probably thinking of his grave and not his house."

The carriage trundled on, and Marjorie, doubting she would get any other answer, sighed and sat back. If the old man gave balls or even teas, Henrietta would, no doubt, manage interest, for all his age—and Maude would be the same. She tilted her head back. And she would, too, she had to admit. Her parents would never free her from Maude's—tutelage until she married. However many years that took. And she would spend all of them with her hair dyed black.

For a moment, she frowned, remembering something about her dead cousin, her husband, and his great-grandfather. But it did not come clearly to her.

"Look," said Henrietta, "beggars." She pointed out a crossroads ahead, at drab, ragged figures there. "They're always there. We shall have to be careful." She turned a triumphant smile on Marjorie.

"Of course we shall," said Maude, sedately.

Marjorie looked at her hands, not willing to look up at Henrietta's smirk.

"We know this is a danger," said Henrietta, leading forward. "Taking you to the riverside. But we will watch you. In case some child falls in—"

"And *watch*," said Marjorie, "is *all* you will do. You won't stop me. And I will come back to drip all over you and all over the carriage, and all your newly purchased finery." She leaned forward. "And get you so wet you will sicken for the rest of the season."

Henrietta gaped as if she had forgotten how to close her mouth. Lady Maude watched Marjorie, and Marjorie had to fight to keep from looking away, like a child who had just stolen jam.

The carriage trundled to a halt, jolting her from her thoughts. By the riverside, a building rose not from the bank but from the river, and the very wood of it seemed green. Maude and Henrietta set out briskly from the carriage, and Marjorie, having no wish to look a country chit, hurried with them.

Inside, great racks held every color of clothing, every ribbon, in lace or a band, every kind of button and notion, with customers scuttling among them. Slim, willowy woman, supple and as brown as river water, flourished their fares so that the air seemed filled with them, like a cascade of flowers at a May festival, and all the fancy ladies nodded gravely and discussed merits of this shade or that. Marjorie managed to walk several steps from the door, but no farther, before she stopped to gawk like a country chit.

"My lady!" One woman came up to her. Her skin had more than a touch of green to it, and her dark eyes glanced over Marjorie and glinted like a river wave in the sun. "You will need gowns for your season here." Maude and Henrietta came up behind her—Henrietta looking as if she had bitten something sour—and Marjorie nodded.

"You have come to the right place." She smiled. "All honest mirrors here—not so magical as Lady Shulamith's—because we have only to show you the truth!"

Cloth and ribbon floated about her, Maude insisting on this, or scornfully dismissing that, without letting Marjorie speak so much as a word, until Maude proclaimed it done and paid out

the coins. A thin little girl scooped up the cloth to lug it out to the carriage. Maude had purchased some things for Henrietta, but the bulk of it—Marjorie stared at the heap—was hers.

The girl flumped the package down in the carriage and grinned, gap-toothed, at Marjorie. "You'll have a dress like springtime."

"So you will," said Maude, ushering her charges inside the carriage. "Tonight, for Lady Celestine's. One night's waiting was enough. If we sew with enough speed, we will have a gown ready for you." Her mouth twisted. "And you will have proof of your sewing skill, if a bridegroom, or his mother, insists on that."

Henrietta pouted. Maude turned on her.

"And, yes, you must sew on it as well. Sew your own tomorrow. It will not even help you by contrast. If they see that your godmother can not fitly prepare her niece, it will reflect poorly on *you*."

Without another word, Maude leaned back against the seat and closed her eyes. Henrietta looked banefully at Marjorie as the carriage trundled along the street, stopping, turning, and climbing hills. A flight of sparrows twittered, swirling about the carriage, and then upward towards the sun. A girl at Queen Hesione's school looked out the window toward them, and leaned forward to see the street and the carriage, and sighed.

"They went to get cloth for ball gowns," she pronounced. "They will go to Queen Shulamith's ball in them."

Her gaze came back to the room. It moved over the book before her, without taking in the words, to settle on her own sleeve, the drab brown of the upper girls' uniform.

"She won't hold a ball when we can go," she pronounced.

"Like we should, Lucy," said Carol, sternly. "No one knows much about Queen Shulamith—not even what kingdom she came from—and look at the wild stories about her mirrors—how can they even know she's a queen, really?"

"Well, it's rude to pry," said Lucy.

"So many exiles," chimed in young Mariana. "And all their sad stories. It's so very rude to question a royal lady and recall all her woes to her."

All the girls bobbed their heads—how tragic that would be, to cause such sorrow to such a highborn and elegant queen—and Carol muttered, under her breath, "A *rich* royal lady."

"She looks like a queen," said Mariana. "All regal and stately, and—queenly."

Carol laughed, shortly. "Like an actress playing a queen. You'd think Queen Tatiana wasn't a queen, all short and squat and with her ugly face all set in mean lines and dressing up in lace and fur so she looks like a pillow—but she's a queen. Only in penny dreadfuls is a queen in exile always young and lovely and sad."

"But—"said Nina, slowly and dreamily emerging from her book, "don't you know, usually? You don't have to ask them. Their servants talk to the butcher, the flower girl, the milkman—bits and pieces, it all comes out."

Lucy nodded. "We heard that Queen Jane's kingdom was offering her the crown back—with a constitution, but still a crown—'cause only a monarch would let them to enter *here*, the City, with ambassadors and everything." She tilted her head to one side. "Her servants talked to *everyone*."

"*Hers* don't," said Carol, portentously. "Queen Shulamith's servants hold their tongues as if Queen Shulamith had them witched—and who ever heard of a queen who was a witch, too?"

"A student who read her history, young Carol," said Queen Hesione, crisply, from the doorway. "If you have so much time to gab, perhaps we should move more briskly. I do not wish your parents to complain that you are not learning so swiftly as you could, when you have so much to learn."

She walked into the room, turning her gaze on Carol. "With what you have said, I must begin at the beginning—do you even know how the city came to be? Who was so silly as to build a city for those who fled their native lands?"

Carol's tongue felt like lead in her mouth. "It wasn't," she stammered. "For exiles. It was for kings. It was magic—they could all come to it with a day's journey, and they did to make peace. So—" She drew a deep breath, and the words came more clearly. "They came again and again. When they had make treaties. Or when they wanted to show off their sons and daughters, for marriages. It was only when there were wars driving them off that they came here as exiles. And when there were *revolutions*, they came. Lots and lots and lots."

Queen Hesione looked a little pale, as if she had not realized this would remind her of her own midnight escape to here, but her voice was cold and clear.

"And so—how do we know that Queen Shulamith is a queen indeed?"

Carol's mouth opened and shut. Finally, she said, weakly, "Because she's here?"

Queen Hesione raised an eyebrow.

"She wouldn't be able to find her way here without royal blood," said Carol, slowly. "They didn't want impostors, or assassins." She started to ponder how the city and its enchantments had managed when kingdoms had changed dynasties.

"Unless she came in an entourage," said Lucy, brightly. "Not everyone here's a king or queen." She spread her hands, having just enough tact not to mention the students did not all have royal blood. "A whole city full of people working—they couldn't all be kings or queens."

Swallows twittered outside, perching on the carvings of ribbons and bows. As the girls recited on, the swallows took wing, flying up and

about, and swirling about the houses where seamstresses and daughters
bent over fine gowns, and mothers standing over them, urging that now
of all times, they had to be proper for every ball—else, they might not
be invited to Queen Shulamith's ball.

At the little taverns at the corners, messengers chortled over how
much gold was to be found, with all the letters flying about, making
plans for the ball.

"Just wait until Queen Shulamith sends her invitations," said one
messenger. "She'll hire messengers right and left."

"Huh," said an old man, perched by the fire place that held only ash-
es. "They don't send 'em like that unless they've got no messengers of
their own."

"She doesn't," the messenger assured him. "When have you heard of
any message from her establishment?"

"When have you heard anything of her servants?" said the tavern-
keeper's daughter, as she filled another mug. "She has them—but nothing's been heard of them."

"Not even," said one man, looking up from his cup, "rumors. You'd
think someone'd claim to have been told by a friend of a friend of something someone said."

The messenger fell silent with the rest. A flight of sparrows twittered by the store, and rising and sinking, they flew down the streets,
until they flew around the preparations at Lady Celestine's, and the upper room where Lady Celestine listened as her daughter Giselle com-
plained.

"They all care only about Queen Shulamith's ball, as if they even
knew anything about what sort of balls she would give—as if there
aren't twenty balls a month—as if it might not be the most tedious
thing that the city could offer." Giselle wrung her hands. "And I want. .
. ."

"No man will want to marry you," said Lady Celestine coldly, "if you
stand about and whine. Go and see to the decorations." She swept off.

Giselle watched her go and, feeling flat, descended the stairs. One worker draping a red rose garland over the arched doorway noticed her and groaned, jabbing his elbow toward the woman for the benefit of the others. They bent their attention back to the garland, intent as if they had never seen the daughter of the house, hoping she would only pass by them instead of giving more orders.

She floated by.

Other workers, with other garlands, went grumbling out to hang more on the walls. And more. And still more as sparrows twittered about them. The mass of the garlands was so great that the workers barely had time to scramble down the ladders and bear them away as the first carriages trundled up. Followed by many more. The stream of them spread out so far that Marjorie could see them from the window.

"Come along," said Lady Maude, without glancing at her, and Marjorie gathered her skirts and followed.

The gown itself, which they had gotten done in time, was pleasant enough, rosy and green, but Marjorie did not look forward to the fittings for the other fabrics, even while they walked to the carriage as the first stars came out in the violet velvet of the sky, and it bore them down the streets to Lady Celestine's.

Lady Celestine herself, her hair silvery-white and her gown blue with silver threads woven through it, came to greet them and exclaim over how striking Maude's charges were before she led them into a room glowing with candles. It reminded Marjorie of many a party she had attended even before they sent her here. The thought did not calm her.

She took the filigree chair Lady Celestine offered here, a chair so delicate and intricate that she did not dare sit back. Perched there, she chatted with the others, telling them about her journey here and eating the dainty comfits that Lady Celestine's servants brought about.

More people glanced across the room and talked about her—Lady Marjorie, Lady Maude's niece, sent here by her parents—some disgrace? or did she live in some countrified corner?

"Not," said one lady, over her cup, "that she could perhaps find a better bridegroom here. Young gentlemen want gracious and prudent wives, ones who will not disgrace them by their lumpish country ways."

Her companion smirked. "And she dyed her hair, no doubt. Such childishness."

"Hardly," said the first, with more gravity. "Only a fool would dye her hair *such* a shade. Blond, the boys like the fair-haired ones."

A snort answered her, and a voice that carried clearly. "The *boys*, yes. Any prudent woman will take care to avoid such boys."

Silvio, new come to the party, eased past the gossips to see the woman they talked of. Easy enough to pick her out: every other woman in the room had long lived in the city, and attended half a dozen balls that he had had to squire them at.

"The new woman—rather pretty," he said to his cousin.

Luc eyed Marjorie for longer, and Silvio's mouth twitched.

"Rather pretty," Luc agreed. "Though it's odd to see such pale eyes with such—dark hair."

Silvio smirked. And then he heard a squeal behind him.

"Silvio!" His young cousin Nina threw her arms about him, and he kissed and greeted her and wondered aloud that her mother had let so young a girl attend parties. Then, the posy of bright-eyed girls, about the same age, flooded about the two of them with exclamations of how glad they were to see them.

"Though," said one, "we *wonder*." Her mouth pursed. "We see you so seldom, we wonder what you are about in the city."

Silvio threw his hand in the air. The lace fell back from his wrist. "To be sure, we have things to do besides gawk at the ladies—even in this city, we are still young cavaliers."

"Though," said Luc, dryly, "we do not get into as many fights as we might, back home."

"An insult!" said Silvio. "Sir, I demand satisfaction!"

Luc looked at his side, where no sword hung, and his mouth twisted. The girls laughed, their hands going up to their faces, but behind them, older guests scowled.

Celestine's cousin Aurore came through the crowd. Her delicate little face was set in firm lines.

"Now that you have amused us all for a moment, you must come and meet my cousin Marjorie. New arrived in the city—and you would rather gad about with conjured swords, or hunt something up in a storeroom! Making her think we are all ready to take to the streets in a troupe as soon as our king is deposed!"

Silvio smiled but followed as well. Luc said, "Is she Celestine's cousin as well?"

"No," said Aurore. "A second cousin, on my mother's side." She bustled them through the crowd, which subsided back to their gossip (however much the two of them would feature in it), and Marjorie politely rose to greet them. Silvio flourished his bow as elegantly as he would have danced—or fought a duel.

Luc thought he could hardly match Silvio's verve—but at least he could assure his father that he had made an effort to meet marriageable ladies, even if he had not won a post with a king. There being no point in wasting his trip here, even if it was the done thing for a young man.

Luc bowed over her hand and straightened. After a moment, she raised an eyebrow.

He nearly blushed. He had not moved at all—"I beg your pardon, my lady, I was noting your eyes. Such an uncommon shade of hazel: almost golden."

Marjorie laughed, shortly. Her companion pursed her mouth, her sour expression not faltering beneath her masses of curls. Luc nodded to her. Henrietta, he recalled.

"Her lovely eyes," Henrietta murmured. "How familiar."

"It is as old as ladies' lovely eyes," said Luc, and Marjorie laughed again, more naturally.

Aurore smiled. "My cousin sent for that woman, Gemma, to entertain us. She should arrive at any moment—you will see that you have nothing like it outside the city."

Marjorie's smile seemed a little wry. Moments later, a bustle by the backdoor declared the arrival, and people drifted toward the room.

"Will there be dancing after?" said Henrietta.

"Only if this—Gemma and her bear do not overawe us all," said Aurore, "and make us fear to emulate them."

Luc snorted. A dancing bear overawing them—he knew how the exiles of society took to fancies. He offered Marjorie his arm. Silvio blinked, and then offered Aurore his. Henrietta pouted and trailed behind as they walked over, and into the candlelit room.

"It is worth seeing," said Marjorie, meditatively. "I have seen her dancing on the streets—and at other balls."

Luc raised an eyebrow.

"Every ball I've attended at the city, in fact."

He forced a chuckle. "A popular sight, then, I must see the spectacle before I seem a bumpkin, not having witnessed—" And then they were in the room itself, and he fell silent.

The bear's brown fur gleamed by the candlelight. The woman beside him flamed in her red gown. Her pale face gleamed beside her black hair as she looked about the room. Her gaze settled on the musicians.

They stirred themselves to play, a delicate little tune. Gemma turned to the bear, which rose on its hind legs and bowed deeply to her. She curtsied as deeply in return.

Luc's eyebrows went up. "That's more than you expect from a dancing bear," he whispered to Silvio. Silvio grunted, not looking away. Luc stepped back to whisper the same to Marjorie. Slowly, she nodded.

Hand just touching paw, bear and woman moved through the measures of the intricate dance. The crowd about them thickened with more and more of those attending, but neither dancer let that perturb their steps.

When the dance ended, the woman curtsied, the bear bowed, and the watchers applauded with enthusiasm.

From the crowd came Lady Celestine's cool, amused voice. "Since it so pleases you, let us have another." Again Gemma curtsied, and the bear bowed. Lady Celestine nodded to the musicians, who struck up a merrier tune, and Gemma and the bear danced again, with nimble steps as they twirled about each other.

"She had best not let it go on too long," said Marjorie to Luc, softly. "We will be overawed and unwilling to dance ourselves for fear of contrast. There must be dancers here who would fear to fall below the bear's skill."

Silvio's mouth twitched as Gemma swirled about, her skirt flaring. Many a dancer in the city would be wise to find the contrast disheartening. But the clumsiest ones, and the heaviest on foot, would continue to dance on everyone else's toes; if they could be discouraged, they would have been.

Lady Celestine called for a third dance, and Gemma and the bear moved through a stately one, but after it, Lady Celestine spoke of their all taking to the dance floor. Gemma collected her coins and angled off with the bear, toward some back door. Silvio heard Luc asking Marjorie to dance, behind him. Many a woman, standing there, could dance with him, but Silvio angled off himself. Behind the dancing room, two pale stairs lead down to the doorway; they curved around into shadow, but the dancing music still reached down there. Gemma walked down one stair, and Silvio, hurrying a little, darted down the other to reach the landing before her.

Gemma started and climbed back up a stair. The bear growled, and its ivory teeth were large and sharp.

Silvio bowed, deeply. "Forgive me, my lady. But be assured I mean no harm." He smiled, though it felt forced even to him. "Your—chaperon surely would keep you safe from any harm."

Gemma snorted, eyeing him.

"Such an admirable dancer. Listen: the dance begins." He held out a hand. "If you humor an impudent rascal, you make escape with nothing more than a trodden on toe, if he proves a worse dancer than your usual companion."

The bear growled. Gemma eyed the door. Still, she held out her hand. Silvio, grinning, took it, and led her into the graceful measures. The bear lurked on the stairs, watching them move in and out of shadow. Gemma even smiled after a minute: impudence was all she could fault in him; he danced more elegantly than many a dancer master she had had.

The music ended. For a moment, Silvio stood there, holding her hand. Then he freed it and bowed. "I shall return to the rest of the dancers, my lady—spoiled for them—you dance as exquisitely as—one would think you learned at court."

Gemma wondered how she managed a smile, but she felt her face move, however stiffly. Though she doubted she could betray more. If he knew—if he even guessed—that she had come from a court, she could only hope that his honor would make him hold his tongue.

He went up the stairs to where the next tune began, back into the candlelight.

Gemma drew in a deep breath. Voices slipped down the stairs.

"Oh so fancy," said one, full of venom. "Like she knows nothing but entertaining the high-born. But you'll see her dancing on the streets come morning for any beggar's brat. Gold, gold, gold—she thinks nothing but of gold!"

A deep, full laugh followed. "And you begrudge her? She will need every coin she can get. She entertains every ball. She is in fashion. Once she is out—I hope she's wise enough to save, she'll be out one day soon."

Her breath gushed out. Coin was one thing, but—she went down to the door, her heart hammering, and the bear on her heels—if she went out of fashion before Queen Shulamith's ball, both the balls and the streets were in vain. She would need to find some other way in. Her mouth tightened. Perhaps the threat of being mauled by a bear, if it came to that.

The door opened, they hurried outside, the door closed behind them, and as it shut out even the little light of the stairway, the bear growled, "What was he up to?"

For a moment, she blinked. He? The money—and her thoughts fell into place.

Her heart still hammering, Gemma turned from the door. He must be worried, to speak so close to the place. "Mischief," she croaked. "The city is full of them. Young men, exiles, or escapees from their father's houses, with no duties." She let out her breath. "Some of them have money enough for it."

The bear's voice deepened. "And no honor, to plague you so. When you could not face him at law."

"He could have done much, much worse," said Gemma. She hurried from the building, to where light spattered on the pavement from the windows, and looked back up. "See, there he is." She gestured up. The light by the window let her see inside, where Silvio laughed with an old woman. The bear eyed him dubiously, but the young man did not even notice him, lost in the shadows below, when he had his social duties to perform. At least the mirth of dancing with Gemma would make the rest less tedious.

Lady Dagmar patted him on the hand. "I know you, young Silvio. You are here to see how many hearts you can break."

"You know me too well, Lady Dagmar," said Silvio. "Though I do not feel guilty enough to become a hermit yet, perhaps I should leave, surrender my share of these festivities, to mortify my mean-spirited desire."

Dagmar chortled. "And you do not know me at all if you think I can not see when you have grown weary of a party!"

Silvio smiled, but his gaze went about the room. Luc stood opposite, with all the dancers between them. He did not look to break hearts, let alone escape the city by marrying well; he did not talk to, let alone flirt with, the woman by him. Then Silvio marked how his gaze followed Marjorie as she moved through the measures. His eyebrows went up. Luc flirted very badly, and had never been one to fall in love every springtide. He nodded to Lady Dagmar and eased his way about the party. He took up a glass of wine, to ease his throat and disguise his purpose, but only exchanged greetings and walked on. Luc, no doubt, would work out whether he wished to marry her without squiring Marjorie to every dance.

Luc looked over as he approached.

"We should leave before we wear out our welcome, perhaps," said Silvio.

Luc looked back at Marjorie—but here, two dances with the same lady would never be permitted. Silvio's mouth twisted. Luc looked like he would chafe at only three, at a ball, but he shook his head and looked away, determined.

"Let us go," he said. After a moment, he smiled. "Is there any reason to go by the streets?"

Silvio considered and glanced about. If they went into that room—"No, there isn't." He drained his glass and put it aside.

Luc led the way through the crowd, smiling and exchanging greetings, but not stopping. He caught Marjorie's gaze to bow his farewell; Silvio, smiling wryly, also bowed, and Marjorie inclined her head. She shouldn't have dyed her hair that color, he thought, it did not become her. Dismissing her from his thoughts, he followed Luc out of the great hall and the candlelight.

The side doorway led them into a room lit only by the stray candlelight from the party. Windows, as tall as a man, arched up, showing the building outside—another house, without its windows so lit—and a sky of a deep purple. Luc picked one window and opened it. A cart rumbled by, far below, but he looked at the roof, overhead.

"Best one?" said Silvio.

Luc nodded, and reached up. If they had not been on the highest floor already, they would have had to find their way to the attic, but here, Luc's fingers bit the eaves, and he swung himself up. Silvio came closer—this was always the tricky part—but with Luc on the roof, he scrambled up to join him.

The house had shielded the sunset, which still gleamed in the west—but only the darkest shades of red and indigo. The gabled buildings were dark against it.

On the roof itself, Silvio moved with more ease. Light-footed, he climbed up to the gable.

"The view isn't that much better up here," said Luc, "and if we are leaving, we should leave." He ran along the rooftop and leapt to the next house. Silvio, laughing, ran after.

The houses on this street were simple enough—of a height, and without large gardens at their sides. But the street ahead was wider than many. Luc ran the faster, and leapt, and the great, easy arc bore him up and over. Silvio thought he heard a squeak from the street below before he hurtled himself over the gap. He laughed. A newcomer to the city, who did not know why people carefully locked their upper story windows in this city, or that a man walking with care was in more danger than one running.

They could prevent anyone without royal or noble blood from using their escape routes, but for those who had it, the paths were easy enough.

Luc had already leapt off, heading along High Street. The straightest route back to his rooms. Silvio's eyebrows went up, and he chased after.

"Eager to be home?" he said, dryly.

Luc glanced sideways at him. "If you don't think you're up to it—" He ran again. Silvio chased him as up the streets. At one corner, a solemn young man glowed as he strummed his lute, and sang below a single lit window, without a shadow showing at it. He must have enchanted himself for this serenade.

They leapt from his beloved's home to the next building, and he gawked, the lute producing a tangle of notes. Silvio laughed, on the other side. "That's no way to win a love, fumbling like that."

Luc smiled. "No telling. Have you never seen a woman cooing over the man who lost on a fight on her behalf?"

Silvio snorted and ran on. Luc chased him, and they bounded up to the library.

There, great glass windows filled the skylights, showing the round tower, the shelves of books on every floor, the pale birds that flew across the open air. Silvio and Luc leapt the glass as well, giving no more heed to their flight than the birds did to them, though one had flown to the books at the very height, right under their path. She wrestled out a book with her beak, took it in her claws, and began the slow circle down, through air smelling faintly of paper.

She reached the floor; still in the air, she transformed. A pale woman in pale robes held the book. A thin figure, swathed in a black cloak, his head covered with a dark hood that shadowed his face, stepped eagerly forward. The librarian bowed her head and gave the book into his hands. He scuttled off. She stood there, shaking her head.

"Really," murmured another librarian by her ear, "those spies never even think to put those impossible cloaks in brilliant colors. You don't even have to wait until they ask for one of those books."

"I've seen them in green," she said. "Or blue."

"But dark of either shade, which is not much help." The other librarian shook her head. "I'm afraid that the news will be all over the city at dawn."

The librarian snorted. "It will never take that long."

As the spy scuttled down the steps, the servants out on midnight errands, and the craftsmen at work in their shops for orders that had to be delivered the next day, looked up long enough to see him, and the excited whispers began. A spy—it was likely that there would be an invasion, and all the streets echoed with the news.

One baker cuffed his apprentices back to work with the comment that they should wonder over Queen Shulamith's ball instead. "She's never had a ball before, but even the youngest of you have seen an invasion."

"But we're not baking for Queen Shulamith's ball," said the youngest apprentice, with flour over him like the dirt of the wooer secretly living as a gardener before he fights for the princess's hand in the tourney.

The baker clouted him, sending the flour flying. "Just because you're the youngest of three princes, you still work here *baking bread*, not *talking nonsense*." He harrumphed and turned away, and the rumors rippled around the bakery. A tailor's apprentices walked by, having to refuse to buy pastries before they delivered the clothes they had finished, and walked on, wondering who the invaders were, and whether anyone in the city knew them.

"They don't always invade on the excuse that someone's taken refuge here," said the younger.

The older apprentice shook his head. "They don't need to."

"Well, yes." The younger one hitched up the black clothing in his arms. "They just say that the city lies within their realm and was seized— " He tried to wave his hand in the air and desperately clutched the clothing. "Like there's anyone in the city who controlled it *now*."

The older shook his head. They turned a corner. "They don't have to *realize* they know someone in the city. There's too many people here. I don't think there's any lands where *someone* hasn't run away to come here." The gates of the house appeared ahead of them. "It's not called the city of exiles for nothing. . . ."

They both stared at those pale steps, with the snow leopard slumbering on them. The older apprentice did not wonder that the master had sent them and not come himself.

The curtains on a window twitched. Though neither prentice looked up, they were clearly seen on the street.

"It's the tailor's 'prentices," said Michel. "With our new clothes."

Philippe, slumped against the hearth, shook his head. "Don't want to."

Michel stepped closer.

Philippe looked up and pouted. "Great-great-grandpa never sees us. Never sees what we wear."

"He'll see *them*," said Michel gloomily. He left the room and went down the long corridor. His footsteps echoed, faintly. After a minute, he heard Philippe's, behind him; he started down the winding stairway, and Philippe's feet pattered as he ran to catch up.

He opened the door to the outside. The apprentices looked up. They gawked at him, and then glanced behind him. When only Philippe appeared there, the older one swallowed and said, "We've got the clothes."

Michel held the door open wide. The apprentices eyed the snow leopard and edged up the stairs, keeping as wide a berth as they could. Across the street, six golden horses, drawing a golden carriage, pranced up to the house. A company of soldiers in green and gold surrounded it.

"Which way do the wardrobes lie?" said the older apprentice sharply. Michel looked up at him; his face was vague, and the apprentice felt a pang. The boys looked less lively than when they had arrived at the tailor's. Perhaps they felt their parents' death more.

That wasn't his fault, and there weren't even any servants here to take charge of the clothing. Would serve the lord right if they laid them down in the hallway. But when Michel led them off, the apprentices followed.

And perhaps news would enliven them. "Have you heard of the invasion?" he asked as they climbed the stairs.

"Invasion?" said Michel, stupidly.

"Cross the street?" said Philippe. When the older apprentice looked at him, astounded at so silly a question, Philippe added, "Soldiers."

Both the prentices laughed, though the sound was strangely muffled, dying off without resounding through the corridors. Neither one quite liked the noise.

The younger prentice said, quickly, "No one would be fool enough to try to conquer the city with that few soldiers."

"Though only a fool would try with any number," said the older one, with relish. When the boys looked back in incomprehension, he looked about. "Where are the wardrobes?"

Michel led on. The prentices followed them down the corridor, hung the clothing in the wardrobe, said that it was just as well that neither of them were old enough to go to Queen Shulamith's ball, with only mourning to wear, and went out to find those who could talk of the invasion.

Michel followed them down to close the door and looked across the street. Both the horses and the carriage had vanished, leaving only the drab front of the house.

"Play in the garden?" said Philippe.

After a moment, Michel nodded. They wouldn't even have to change. Even Great-Great-Grandfather couldn't complain if they didn't wear mourning when they weren't going about the city.

"In the back garden," he said.

They wandered down back stairs, narrow and steep, not meant for lordly types, and reached the marble of the garden, under a sky covered with dove-gray clouds. Some plants grew scattered about the stones: rosebushes as tangled as the trees, with a few pale blooms, and more dark thorns than they had leaves. Philippe stared up at one glowering statue of a hairy man with a bull's head but went on when Michel tugged on his hand, and they came to broad stairs, leading down to a pool. A pool that held goldfish, some as small as Philippe's thumb, some as long and thick as Michel's forearm, all of them as pale as ghosts—some tinged with gold, others with spots of flaming orange, still others with nothing at all, only bone-white scales.

"Ghosts of goldfish," said Michel, "they're still gold."

Philippe scowled, and Michel half-agreed. A gold like cream, almost white—"We should get bread from the kitchen, and feed them the crumbs."

Philippe looked up, almost bright-eyed.

"We could lure them up from the depths."

"Oooo!" said Philippe, and Michel smiled back at him. They could see if all the fish were as pale as those they could see.

"Could you now?"

The woman's voice was cold and—dusty, though Michel. Philippe looked at him with enormous eyes, and they both turned toward the stairs.

A woman stood at the top of the stairs. Her face and hair and clothing all were pale brown that was almost gray in drabness, and she was so round that Michel thought of river rocks, piled on each other.

She looked from one to the other of them with her pale eyes. "Shush, both of you," she said. "And no mischief about bread." She went down a couple of the stairs, and then fluttered her hands at them. "Be off with you."

Philippe grabbed Michel's hand. Michel led him off, up the stairs opposite the woman. He could almost feel the woman's eyes on his back as they climbed, but he did not want to look back and slow himself.

"She *scares* me," whispered Philippe.

"She's scary," whispered Michel. "But we won't feed the fish, and she won't. . . ."

Philippe's nose twitched. "She's so fat, she wants to eat all the bread *herself.*"

Michel giggled, and they ran up the last steps. More statues stood about, several of them looking balefully down, but one slender woman raised her arms up and arched her wings through the air. Michel scurried over to her, and looked up at the statue. Philippe looked with wide eyes.

Brighter than anything else in the garden, as red as roses or a sunset, birds flitted over the statue's hands.

"She's not going catch them like that," said Michel. Philippe giggled, and started to laugh, and Michel joined him. The laughter rang from the stones. All about, things stilled, even the fish in the pond, and from statuary and all the carvings on the house, eyes looked at them, and the house glowered.

The laughter carried out of the garden, all the same, and across the way where schoolgirls walked to Queen Hesione's school and talked of what they would have worn to Queen Shulamith's ball, and how it would have looked in her enchanted mirrors, to an open window across the way, where Reinette, frowning, looked up from her jewelry.

"I had thought this quarter held no children," she said, snipping out each word. "I had thought it had been chosen for that."

"There weren't," said Augusta. "It had been. But such things happen—Your Majesty."

Reinette scowled and sat back. That was no tone to take to the queen, even if you were her mother. She picked up a string of pearls, and then let it dribble through her fingers. Not that her mother would listen. It seemed unregal to scold, especially to no effect. She was a queen and not a fishwife.

"You must concentrate on finding a suitable bridegroom," said Augusta. "There are too many nobles here. They will try as earnestly as any fool back home to lure you into an unequal match, and here they have many more ways to hide their birth."

As bad as Queen Lenore was, thought Reinette. "I must prepare, then, and so it is time to go for ribbons."

Augusta paused, and Reinette smiled. For once she had taken her aback.

"It's—look at the clouds," said Augusta. "It will *rain*."

"You talk as if I would go on *foot*, like some thread-bare princess who slaves in a kitchen," said Reinette. "I will go in the carriage, of course, and properly attended. I know that no one respects royalty who do not keep proper state. By the same token, I can hardly be so *countrified* as to wear ribbons from home."

She swept off, calling for servants. They leapt up from their chatter—all about this nonsense about an invasion or some queen's ball. She didn't pay them to prattle about such commonplaces. Her commands snapped out, and they flew for her mantle, to harness the horses, to lead out her carriage.

When it glittered before the house, with the horses in their golden harness, Augusta stood by the front door, her mantle over her shoulders, her face as calm as though she had proposed the expedition.

Reinette nodded to her. It would hardly do to leave her behind. For all the perils of matrimony, whether an equal match or an inferior one (since she had no superiors to wed), at least no one would claim she need her mother to chaperon her once she married. Until then, a queen could not go so unattended as a milkmaid.

Reinette climbed into the carriage on her own and settled on the purple velvet of the seats. The groom helped Augusta up after her. Reinette cast her a sidelong glance. That, after all, had long been Augusta's aim: to make her daughter the queen, and so her superior.

The carriage lumbered off and down the narrow streets. It rose up the slope to High Street, and Alixandre, over tea, said, "Why, there she is." As the others glanced, "The carriage is that of Queen Reinette. Queen Lenore's niece."

"Oh, yes," said Blanca, without rising to look out the window. "Queen Lenore was truly foolish to have given birth to a bear. Now she is merely the queen dowager, and not the queen mother."

Ida shook her head, pouring more tea. She reached for the honey. "I don't imagine that there was actually a law against a bear succeeding."

Alixandre snorted. "Hardly needs to be one." Her gaze went back to the carriage. It rolled on, far beneath them, toward the river, through a welter of towering buildings that loomed over it with unreadable windows looking down but reflecting only the scene before them.

Augusta gave those windows a glance before she said, "I can not imagine that this is the quickest route. Not when we had to go up so high. . . ."

"But look," said Reinette, "there is the river."

Wider than some lakes she had seen, the river glinted back the sky's gray, and in the shadow of the waves, rolled darkly along. One could hardly mistake the shop, not with all the carriages by it, and the liveried grooms playing at dice, and the gentlemen talking of how their wives, or daughters, or sweethearts, shopped. In fact—Reinette's eyes narrowed—she could hardly mistake some of those gentlemen. Her mouth felt sour. Nobles who fled to the City of Exiles as if they had reason to fear her. . . .

When the carriage stopped, and the groom opened the door, Reinette sat still. She almost wished she had dressed more regally, but retreating home would hardly impress them. The groom held out his hand, and Reinette took it to descend.

At least they recognized her. Both Luc and Silvio bowed.

Reinette smiled. "How odd to find you here. I had not thought that either of you had any reason to flee my kingdom—nor that you were such fops and dandies as to shop here."

"Here?" said Silvio. He straightened, as if about to put his hand to his sword. "We are escorting a goddaughter of my mother's cousin."

"But then," said Reinette, "such a task makes your flight more puzzling." She took out her fan to fan herself and hide half her face while she studied them. "Surely you know you could not have fallen into your godmother's power, letting her assign you such feats, if you had remained home."

Silvio shrugged. "But, Your Majesty, we were chased from your kingdom—by—by our own youth and love of adventure! You must concede that the marvels here allure young men."

"Our fathers drive us into exile," said Luc, "so we will disgrace ourselves in foreign lands rather than where their reputations will suffer." His smile, unsurprisingly, did not reach his eyes; he had mastered that much of being a courtier.

"I know that young men love adventure," said Reinette. "That is why they go to the forests to hunt."

"Only some of them," said Luc. "Some of us are such fops and flirts that we can not bear such isolation." He bowed again. "Doubtlessly, Your Majesty, we will see you in all your finery at the city's festivities."

"And this store shall provide them to us," said Augusta, stepping forward. Her eyes were narrowed, and her mouth pursed. Reinette scowled, but walked with her, and Augusta spat, "Slanging in the street like a fishwife! They will think *nothing* of you."

Reinette gave her a baleful glance—a queen should not have to care what such passers-by thought—and hurried on, into the store. Cloth and ribbons burst to either side, and a slim brown woman, bending like a river reed, looked up.

"Ah—Queen Reinette, is it not?" She smiled, blandly. "I am sure we can find ribbons to please a queen here."

Another woman, her brown hair loose in curls about her shoulder, came toward the door, bearing a basket on her arm. Reinette walked by her without a glance, and Henrietta walked on, to Silvio and Luc.

"Found all you wanted?" said Luc.

"Found everything that we need," said Henrietta, her mouth set in sour lines. "Lady Maude would never consent to buying more than we need for the parties."

Luc rolled his eyes, but Henriette's sour expression did not change. They started up the streets.

"And I would not buy a thread more than we need. She has the maids do *some* of the work, but Lady Marjorie and I have to sew, and sew, and sew. As if some queen mother would decide that the woman who sewed the best would be her daughter-in-law." She arched her neck, and her hair fell free. "Worse today. We are all ready for Queen Shulamith's ball, but she *will* say that it will rain today, and so Lady Marjorie and I must *stick* to our sewing."

"Lady Marjorie," said Luc. "Did you know her before she came here?"

Henrietta slowly straightened and looked at him, narrowing her eyes. "No. I did not." After a minute, she said, "Do you have cousins or unmarried uncles?"

She was quick to presume on invitations to dance. "Silvio's a cousin," Luc said.

Her mouth pursed, and they walked up the street in silence. Silvio deliberately stepped behind Henrietta's back and, casting a sidelong glance at her, cocked an eyebrow at Luc.

Luc shrugged. He had done nothing to encourage her, at any rate, and they could deliver her back to Lady Maude. It was better here, at least, than at home, where the court ladies of their kin would have them running errands day and night. It would be worse there when Queen Reinette secured her coronation, and no one could escape her whims.

Down a cross-street ran a brown little man, barely reaching the height of Luc's shoulder. He drew a deep breath at the crossroads, glancing about as if to be sure enough people gawked at him.

"The invasion! The invasion's come!"

"The invasion!" It echoed all about. Apprentices looked up from their work, shopkeepers from their counters, vendors from their sales, and Luc's mouth pursed. At the shop next to them, the three daughters begged, and finally, their father let them go.

"Really," said the shopkeeper, "it's not likely that people will go shopping now."

"Really," said Henrietta, pulling her skirt aside as a shopkeeper's daughters hurried by her, "they act as if it's never happened before."

"What," said Luc, "you don't want to go?"

Henrietta's mouth pursed. "Once you've seen one of them, you've seen them all."

"You've seen one before?" said Silvio. "When was the last one? I would have thought you were too young."

Henrietta looked away.

At least, Maude's house lay, visible, ahead, thought Luc. He strode on. Silvio matched his pace, and Henrietta had to hurry to keep up.

With only the briefest thanks, she darted inside, without an invitation in or a glance back. Luc let his breath out.

"Cousins," said Silvio gloomily. He turned away, to where people streamed through the streets. His smile twitched at his mouth. "Then, of course, there's the invasion."

Without another word, they went up the street. Luc calculated buildings and roofs; they were not close to the gates, and a position to see all would not be easy to find in the crowd.

Two women came down the street, against the flow: Marjorie, looking harried, and a maidservant. Luc walked toward them, and Marjorie started.

"Good morning—what is this all?" She turned her hazel eyes—so mismatched with her black hair—toward him. "An invasion? They act more like a troupe has come to the city. And not any old troupe—one with a—" Her hand swept the air. "—entire company of dancing bears with a band to play for them, and talking parrots, and seventeen magicians without peer—not an army!"

Luc smiled. Closer than she knew.

"It's not like they all want to stare at the uniforms. There's only so much you can do with cloth and braid and you can see it on the street every day."

"Yes, it's an invasion," said Luc. No doubt Marjorie could see that no one lugged such treasures as they could carry, seeking to escape. Certainly, no one looked frightened except the smallest of children, and them at the tumult. He doubted his ability to explain it to her. And Silvio looked impatient.

"I was visiting Johanna—she's a cousin who lives here, but poor and ailing—" She pulled back her loose hair from her face. "With all this commotion, she has to rest." She looked back at Luc. "Even Johanna wasn't frightened, and she *couldn't* flee. What is happening?"

Luc drew a deep breath. "Would you like to see?"

The maidservant looked over, sharply. "How could you? It's dangerous—"

Silvio's shout of laughter cut her off.

Marjorie smiled. "I would like to." As soon as Luc held out his arm, she stepped forward to take it. Luc calculated buildings and roofs again. He could not take Marjorie everywhere where his own feet could bear him.

"This is absurd," said the maidservant.

"Of course," said Silvio. "Gabbing while everyone else is going to see—it is far from the most important thing happening in the city, but it is unquestionably the one with the best spectacle—but we shall see nothing, even if we arrive in time, because we will have no position to do it from." He walked off, briskly, and Luc and Marjorie followed. The maidservant scurried after.

"Everyone is fascinated," said Marjorie, her voice low. "How often does this happen, to entrance us all when it does?"

Luc felt his mouth twitch, and confessed, "This is the first time since I've been here. But they say you haven't really been to the City if you have not seen an invasion."

"It can't—they wouldn't—the kings would not have held their parleys here if it were so dangerous."

"Oh no," said Luc. "The invasions only really started after this started to be the city of exiles. But dangerous?"

"Here's a good way," called Silvio, drawing eyes all about. But when the crowd saw how he gestured at a gray alley, scarcely large enough for a single person, most hurried along on the road. Luc walked up. The alleyway twisted ahead of them.

"You're up to some mischief, I know," said the maidservant, wrathfully.

"Only seeing the invasion," said Luc. He had to loose Marjorie's arm for them to hurry through the alleyway, with Marjorie following Silvio, and the maidservant scurried after them all. The walls to either side towered over them—featureless, with no windows as high as they went—and the alley quickly turned into a long flight of narrow stairs, turning here and there so they could not see its height. The top of the walls never seemed to be any closer; between the two, they could see only scraps of cloud. They climbed, and climbed, and an arch bore a passageway overhead, with tiny windows looking down.

"Bet you that can see the invasion from the windows," said Silvio, "but there's no easy way there. Not like—" He strode up seven steps, and about a turn. His voice filled with satisfaction, he said, "Not like this."

Marjorie climbed. About the turn, a wall towered, but it held an arched doorway, and beyond, a balcony from which they could see buildings and clouds. Silvio smiled and handed her through.

From the balcony, the gates were clear to be seen: enormous, high enough to admit an elephant, built of oak so old as to be black, and bound with wrought iron. They opened on the square, now devoid of people. A few birds twittered on the flagstones, pecking here and there at crumbs, flitting about as if they watched the gates. All the stores had put up heavy shutters on their windows, and their doors were shut—heavy oaken doors, doubtlessly bolted. She had seen prisons with doors less secure.

Marjorie let her breath out. Shutters barred the second story windows, and even the third, but the higher windows had people leaning out, and crowds filled the roofs and murmured. Like people expecting a grand parade. With dancing bears—no, they had seen dancing bears on the street. With dancing lions and unicorns.

And there were no barriers set up on any street in.

Marjorie's eyes went back to the gate. No guards, even, stood there.

Luc came up beside her. His hand came up, across her back, to touch her other elbow, and Marjorie looked down at her hands. Muttering ferociously, the maidservant settled by the stairs. Silvio leaned against the balcony.

Marjorie tilted her head to one side. "How many invasions have you seen?" she said to the maidservant.

The maidservant shifted and muttered something about, "Too many."

A great thundering note shook the gate. After a minute, it creaked open. With such twittering cries that they filled the air with noise, the birds leapt upward, their wings beating as they flew for the roofs. A cloud of feathers spread, and sunlight shone through the wings, making the birds luminous.

The gate continued to open, revealing nothing behind it.

"Magic," said Silvio as the gates moved steadily. "More elegant than a battering ram, I suppose."

"Depends on the magic, by all accounts," said Luc.

Marjorie noted what they said, to sound less like a fool at the next ball.

Fully open, the gates admitted files of soldiers, each of them gleaming in blue with gold braid, their polished guns held ready. Their officers, bearing swords, rode on prancing, eager horses, every one of them a fine black.

"Folly," said Silvio, his voice dry. "Matching horses like that is for show, not for war. Their commanders should know that the City is not to be overawed."

"But," said Marjorie, "it is to be taken by force?"

Silvio blinked, and Luc laughed.

"She has you there. Once they choose to invade, it's not a question of prudence or folly, but a choice of follies."

She looked back at the folly in the square. From this distance, she could not see whether the soldiers were taken aback by the emptiness that greeted them. Not until companies had marched within did anyone in the army show any hesitation. An officer shouted a demand for surrender. After a moment, he shouted that the city had always fallen within the borders of the country. She could not make out the name he used. She supposed it did not matter.

Laughter rose from windows all about. Even Luc and Silvio smiled.

Marjorie stirred a little. The officer's face, turned upward, moved as if he were looking for something. "Why doesn't he *look* at them?"

"He can't hear them," said Luc. "Or see them."

"All part of the magic," said Silvio, merrily. "See how he doesn't threaten to *besiege* the city, cutting off our food—and the chances of exiled kings to come here and hide."

Marjorie's mouth curved, a little, but smoothed itself back out. The soldiers shouted taunts; raucous as they were, they lost something, dying out before they echoed far through the streets. Officers marched them on, down streets that seemed narrower, and more dingy and gray, than they had moments earlier.

Marjorie shivered. Luc's arm tightened about her, and she was glad of the warmth.

The streets had been level, she had seen that, but now, the soldiers marched downwards. Streets grew narrower beneath her gaze. Buildings loomed about the men, as tall as the tallest she had seen in the city, or taller. She could see only those who had marched down streets giving her a clear view, away from her. Shadows fell on them. In the begrimed streets, the uniforms no longer shone; the blue seemed almost gray. Streets twisted before them, like a labyrinth, and they turned corners, and were gone.

"I wonder if they can still see them, elsewhere," said Luc.

Marjorie shuddered. "It's horrible, horrible."

Silvio gave her a sideways glance.

"It's an invasion," said Luc. "What they intended—"

Marjorie looked at him. "I doubt their king, or even any of their princes, was one of those gallant officers."

Luc shifted. "They spoke of their country, not their kingdom. Probably some republic trying to seize run-away royalty."

Marjorie swept the air with her hand. "Some president or consul or what have you then—was not one of those gallant officers. I doubt that many soldiers had any choice."

"Dying on the battlefield wouldn't have given them a choice," said Luc. "Neither would their foes' dying there."

Silvio snorted. "Adventure is one thing," he said, "but I have no wish to fight off one of those armies."

Marjorie drew a deep breath, turning away from the balcony. The maid looked up hopefully. Marjorie looked at the stairs, but she said, "Will they vanish?"

"There are tales of bedraggled soldiers making a wild appearance at this party or that," said Luc.

"Going to Queen Shulamith's ball?" said Silvio.

Marjorie blinked. "Is it likely?"

"Possible," said Luc. "Not likely." His mouth twisted. "Certainly no more likely than one or two appearing in Lady Maude's garden."

Laughter suddenly echoed, nearby. Two little boys, in black clothing but bright faced, ran down the balcony. Luc started down the stairs again, and they left the balcony to Michel and Philippe, running along in delight, glad to be free and glad to have seen the soldiers utterly baffled.

"Never escape!" said Philippe, gleefully.

"Never," said Michel, glad that they had listened to the tales on the street of the invasion. They reached the end of the balcony and started down the stairs there. Better than that nasty old house. The streets below were filled with laughing people, rejoicing in their escape.

"Amazing that any of them try it," called one old man, and Michel wandered along the streets with Philippe, and told him about even bigger and bolder soldiers back home, who wore uniforms of purple and gold, much more fitting than the blue these ones wore.

They reached a corner, and Michel stopped, trying to ponder which way to go. He had heard that the city had bad places in it, and he had never seen this place before.

"Where are we going, Michel?" said Philippe.

"Home," said Michel, without hesitation, but he did not move.

"Home, of course," said a deep, disapproving voice, from far over their heads. Michel slowly looked up. Ash-colored, tall and thin like chimney, a man he had never seen before looked down at them with eyes as black as soot. "You will go home at once." Lean hands with fingers like bone came down to take them each by hand. "After all the trouble you brought your great-great-grandfather, to go and vanish like that."

Michel did not quite follow their path through the streets. The man strode along, his legs so long that Michel and Philippe had to scramble to keep up, and panted for breath without his having pity on them. The buildings seemed paler and more drab than any they had seen before. None of them had so much as a window box of flowers, he could barely tell them apart, the people wore dingy clothing and never looked up from the flagstones, and even trying to remember the turns made Michel dizzy.

The first thing he recognized was the gate of his great-great-grand-father's house, and though he hated it again on sight, he walked toward it. He did not know what the tall, thin man could do.

Inside the gate, Michel and Philippe walked toward the door. Behind them, the tall, thin man latched the gate, and then Philippe gasped.

"Where did he go?"

Michel frowned and looked about. The man had latched the gate from the inside, he had seen it, but the garden held no trace of him. He grabbed Philippe's hand. "Let's go inside."

The corridors seemed placid, as if their outing had given them time to calm themselves. They did not let go of each other's hands, wandering along them.

"We got to the invasion," said Philippe. He peered down a side corridor. "And *everyone's* going to Queen Shulamith's ball."

Not boys and girls, thought Michel. Even big boys and girls, and they were still little.

The light that came through the windows ahead left most of the white-washed corridor in shadow; they stood in the gloom.

Philippe rubbed his nose. "The bear lady might be back in the square. With the bear."

With that thought, they ran up the stairs and out on the balcony to look. The woman was indeed there, her scarlet skirt flaring as she and the bear moved through a country dance. Philippe laughed.

"What impudent children you are," said a woman. Michel turned. A thin, short woman, barely taller than Michel, stood in the door to the balcony, which they had left open behind them. Her nose flared, and she walked briskly forward, to take them by the arm and draw them back inside. "Letting drafts into the house like that." She shut the door behind them. And then she was gone as the man had gone.

Michel drew his breath in and let it out. He should have watched the woman by the pool.

He turned to Philippe and said, "We will go to Queen Shulamith's ball." And then he looked about for a window, and they went to watch the bear's dancing through it.

The woman and bear pirouetted through a dainty dance, and coins clattered around them. Gemma kept a careful eye on the money; that kept her face down, hiding her expression. Once inside the ball, she could learn the truth of the mirrors, and it was so close she could taste it—but any noble might be able to keep her out, if he thought she was up to something, or even if he just took a distaste to her. Queen Shulamith would hardly offend a guest of noble blood for the sake of a street entertainer. Who really was of common blood, if it came to that.

With the last measure, Gemma turned to curtsy, far more gracefully than the bear bowed. But—her mouth twisted—it was the bear's bow that brought applause, albeit with laughter and more coins. She stooped to gather up the coinage. Someone would wonder, if she were careless about her pay. Then having gathered it all, she headed toward the park. And admitted to herself that they might need the money as well.

They walked down an almost empty street when the bear growled, "Dancing all day, and then at the ball—"

Gemma glanced at housewives gossiping about a doorway. Did the bear *want* to give them something to gossip about?

"You've done it before," she said, not looking at the bear. "And with a prospect this close, you would be a fool to risk it."

"We don't even know if Queen Shulamith's mirrors will help." Sounding sullen and malcontent.

"Nothing else in the city will, and we will know soon enough," said Gemma. When a handful of schoolgirls slipped out of a side road and chattered on their way to the park, Gemma thanked God. She hurried to keep up with them, and the bear lumbered along, holding its tongue.

If only this would work, the bear would forgive her.

One schoolgirl glanced scornfully over her shoulder, as if disdaining the very thought of watching a dancing bear, so commonplace. Gemma's mouth twitched. At the gate to the park, she took the fork that led to the great lawns. Few people looked at her, and none drew near, but she set up as if she expected a crowd, or as if every coin she might draw was inestimably precious. And then, setting the magic playing the music, she began to dance on the lawn.

The bear lumbered into the measures as if they had not quarreled on the way, and Gemma turned, her skirt swirling. An orange butterfly hung on the air, as if she had shed it. She smiled and turned into the dance, and saw two more butterflies, the sunlight passing through their orange wings and making them glow.

The music held her; she danced on. And perhaps, it was the dance that brought them, as butterfly after butterfly flew up from the ground or in from the lawn and flitted and glowed about them. The bear hesitated now and again, and Gemma did not know how she kept to her step; it was like dancing in the heart of a gemstone.

The music stopped. Gemma stood, panting. Butterflies flew up, and down, and slowly fluttered away, the cloud dispersing over the park. Gemma watched them go. And she had not drawn watchers. There would be no coin. And, with her heart pattering from more than the dance, she did not care what conclusions anyone would draw. Queen Shulamith wanted her at the ball, and she needed nothing else. She gathered up everything again, and started to walk about the park. In the silence, the bear lumbered along with her, down the long paths, under willows by a lake, and up into a corner where oaks stood before the buildings that edged the park.

Gentlemen had gathered by that gate, and Gemma hesitated. Best not to go that far, and tempt fate. After a moment, she stepped closer to the bear. It did not growl, but its shoulders bunched, and it would growl the moment it thought her threatened. Which would tempt those young men. Like every nobleman in the city, they wore swords, and they looked young enough to wish to use them and show their bravery. It was not as if she could take them to court for killing her bear.

She let her breath out. When they were so close—she looked about, for the best path away. They had to start for the ball soon.

A woman shrieked. Gemma's head whipped around. A woman staggered out of an alleyway, into the park. In a fine golden gown—which showed a little dirt, but was not tattered at all. No one followed her out, but her face was pale as bone, color utterly drained form her lips.

"Gentlemen!" Reinette's voice tried to ring, but faltered. "Gentlemen! There are soldiers from the invasion—" She waved back at the alleyway. "They are chasing me!" She stared from face to face. Surely no man of common blood would dare carry a sword, and no man of noble blood would stand aside while riffraff menaced a queen, and above all else a young and lovely queen.

But they did not move—

They even eyed her as she were no more than the dancing girl with her bear.

"Yeah," said one man. "We can hear the footsteps." And at that they all laughed. Some of them eyed her with scorn.

"Ask the bear," shouted another. He waved back at it, standing next to that black-haired woman, the entertainer. "A great fierce bear like that would protect you better."

The woman stepped back. "He must go and dance at Queen Shulamith's ball." She scurried off, without a glance back, her red skirt swirling. The bear lumbered along, and Reinette stared after her, with narrowed eyes. Such impudence.

She remembered the soldiers and started. Looking back, she could not see them, but she could never mistake those blue uniforms, with their gold braid, even torn and filthy and bloodied. She shuddered and fled. When they burst out, the soldiers would find those *gentlemen*, and the soldiers had been too wild and uncaring about whom they attacked to chase after her while they had such foes before them.

And she would never ever—even to hide from her mother—leave the house again without proper state. She drew her breath in and let it out. She would relegate her mother *somewhere*. A tower where they brought up the food by basket might be secure enough. As for reason, she could cook up something. Accuse her of treason, at need. Augusta fought to make her queen. Let her learn that she succeeded, and her daughter would be *queen*. And never have to suffer such insolence again. Neither from *gentlemen* nor from street dancers.

She stalked off, or tried to; she could not keep her path straight. The streets clamored with people. Children ran before her as if they could not imagine caring who she was—children in apprentice's smocks, or with dirty faces and torn clothes.

Reinette looked away, but she was not near enough a wall to block out such sights. And she had come to find a bridegroom here! Perhaps even among those rascals who jeered at her plight! Her mouth tightened. She would never wed. She would remain single forever, and it would serve her kingdom right if her death left them scrambling for an heir. The only reason they supported her claim enough to win her a coronation was their own rivalries: they could not support a single pretender to put her down.

She stormed up the stairs into the house. Servants exclaimed and whirled about, bearing her off like a breeze taking up leaves. Up in her chambers, the women, full of shock and concern, took off her gown to replace it and fussed over whether it could be repaired at all, and over her bruises. Well enough, Reinette thought, begrudgingly. Even in this city, people occasionally knew the respect owed to royalty—

The shatter of glass broke into her thoughts.

Reinette blinked and cast her gaze about. Across the room, a woman—one of the clumsy oafs—cringed over a broken perfume bottle.

Moments later, the room rang from the slap, and Reinette's hand stung. "Go," she spat. "Go at once. You are no longer in my service." She whirled away. "Where is the captain of my guard?"

They fluttered, some of them fleeing and saying that he must know that she would need him, he would be ready to serve her, they would just find him. . . .

He came, a minute later. He looked rather gray, but he bowed, and straightened for her orders.

She fought down a twitch of her lip. They knew her to be just; and she knew that she had evaded his protection. He had no right to act as if she would dismiss him. But if he knew her so poorly, she would not betray her mood to him.

"The woman who dances with the bear in the streets—the black-haired woman, wears a fiery red dress."

The captain nodded.

"She mocked me." Reinette turned a little. "She mocked me this day, and *you* must see to it that she does not run off and dance at Queen Shulamith's ball as if such street tatterdemalions could speak to—"

She cut off her words before she sounded more of a fishwife than she already had. The captain bowed. She let her breath and hoped he did not fall her as badly as that maidservant, as he left the room.

He strode more quickly as soon as he left the room—past the room where other maid servants whispered encouragement to the dismissed one, about how the city held many nobles from their kingdom, she was certain to find a place—and once in the guards' quarters, he shouted for his men and sent them out on the streets. Queen Shulamith's ball—as if the woman, like any entertainer, would not arrive early, long before the ball began.

If they did not find her—he wondered if the men would return to warn him, so that he would know not to return to Queen Reinette's house, himself.

But one, scarcely more than a boy, came running back, over the cobblestones, with the news that they had seen this Gemma walking with her bear toward Queen Shulamith's palace.

"Good," said the captain. A woman foolish enough to mock a queen might indeed be foolish enough to walk so late to the ball. And in the streets of this city, no more safe than any other—less safe than some. He loosened his sword in its scabbard, and summoned the rest to follow him as they walked out on the street. Servants running with packages took one glance at them and darted from their way. Vendors fell silent and pulled into the shelter of an alleyway. Even a querulous old man, walking with a cane and holding the arm of his granddaughter, stopped his rambling long enough to see them, and not walk in their way.

The noise of their footsteps drew Gemma's attention. She glanced over her shoulder, even as the captain saw her and ordered his men to move out. She could see how they eyed her.

The bear snarled, fiercely.

"You can not fight them all," said Gemma. "Run on." She grabbed her skirts, and ran. After a moment, the bear lumbered into a run: awkward, but fearfully fast. The soldiers shouted and ran after. Someone bellowed at them, "What are you doing?" but the ringing footsteps did not hesitate, and no one, of course, stood in the way of armed men.

She ran so quickly that her thoughts were laggard and took minutes to realize that they wore the livery of that woman—who must have taken offense. Her mouth tightened. She had to escape; they would not decide she was too much of a bother to chase.

Not the shops, thought Gemma. No shopkeeper could stand against soldiers. She wished she knew the alleyways here, but she could be trapped as well as escape through one, if she picked the wrong one. The house of nobles stood ahead. The soldiers would not dare—but they shouted and ran after her into those streets. Then, no gentlemen stood about to stop them. . . .

A garden gate opened ahead of her. A black-haired young woman, in green brocade, gestured at her, and Gemma did not hesitate. Especially when the woman was too finely gowned to be a servant.

"Stop her!" bellowed from behind, but Gemma and the bear slid within. The woman—the Lady Marjorie, she had been at the ball—slammed the gate shut and bolted it. A good solid bolt, on a heavy iron gate. The soldiers would have to break through that. If they dared. And if there were no enchantments on it to complicate even that. Gemma stood, panting—the bear was breathing hard itself.

"Come," said Marjorie, and for all that her legs ached, Gemma did not argue as the woman led her and the bear deeper in a rose garden. Flowers brushed their petals against them, red and pink and yellow.

"*Marjorie*!"

Lady Maude towered in the gap between two bushes heavy with blood-red roses, and eyed Marjorie up and down. "When you *knew* your father's wishes—and you have made yourself unfit for the ball!"

Marjorie gaped. She looked at herself, and realized that somehow in that flight, she had torn her sleeve. She looked miserably at it. She would, she supposed, have done the same thing whatever she had known would come of it, but to have accidentally—she felt a fool.

"Perhaps you should address yourself to *sewing*," said Lady Maude. "Perhaps you might manage to make yourself presentable for the ball—in time." She turned, her violet skirts swirling about her, and stalked off.

Certainly not in time, thought Marjorie, miserably. She could not sew well enough to make the tear invisible, and Lady Maude would require it.

She felt a hand on her arm. "Come," said Gemma. "Come deeper into the garden."

Marjorie hesitated, and then took a few steps with her.

Gemma turned to the bear as she walked. "*You*, stay here."

The bear looked at her for a moment, and sat down on its haunches. Gemma whirled Marjorie away, to where the rose bushes hid them from all, and a small bench sat under an arbor of yellow roses.

Gemma said, "Now, take your gown off."

Marjorie eyed her, but then, she had her shift on, under it, and a woman who could make a bear dance like that must be truly odd. Carefully, she unlaced and shed the gown. Then she spread it on the bench. If Gemma could do something about the tear. . . .

Gemma raised her hands and started to move them, swifter and more gracefully than when she danced—and more oddly, too. After a moment, a petal flew off the rose bushes, then, another, and another. They swarmed over the woman, and then Gemma brought her hands down, and the petals flooded over Marjorie, as ticklish as the brush of a bee's wings. But these settled and formed, and Marjorie found herself staring down at an elegant gown, glowing yellow. She moved, hesitantly.

"It will hold," said Gemma. "As good as any woven fabric. Longer than many."

Marjorie eyed the poppy-red of Gemma's skirts, and Gemma smiled. Marjorie let her breath out and took up the brocade gown. With time, she could sew the tiny, careful stitches that would let her wear the gown again, at another ball. For now, before the ball—

"Come with me. Bring your bear."

Gemma's mouth twisted.

At their approach, the bear looked up, and looked as surprised as that furry maw could manage. It lumbered to its feet. Marjorie led them, quickly, through the garden, to a little back gate, and Gemma breathed a sigh of relief. She and the bear walked quickly down the back alleyways to the barn.

"I—" said the bear. "We have to get to the ball."

She had never heard him nervous before. Certainly never so nervous. "I know. Therefore, I will do nothing elaborate. We shall have to run some risks."

She considered the streets a minute. They could choose their path as well. "Stand still," she said, and murmured through a spell. "That will—obfuscate us. They will not know us, if they do not see much of us." She let her breath out. "Come. We must go *now*. The route will be longer."

The bear ambled along, but when she turned down to the river, it slowed for a moment, and then walked closer to her. Every now and again, she felt the brush of his rough fur against her skirts.

"Turn here, by the bridge," she whispered, and stopped. Firelight gilded the bridge's stones. She could not see the fire itself or, worse, who stood about it.

She had walked boldly enough with the bear, through all the roads that had brought them to the city, and all streets that had borne them through it. She walked on. The bear's pace had not slowed; she wondered if he had even noticed her hesitation.

A shrill pipe sounded, and a tune sprung up. A dancing tune, and her feet began to ache already. Gemma set her mouth and walked on, down the stairs. After this night, she could declare herself sick of dancing and never do it again.

A woman danced, a black form against the orange flare of the fire, and nearly as graceful and supple as the flames themselves, dancing in river breezes.

If it hadn't been for the bear, thought Gemma, her own dancing would never have drawn such coins. She kept on walking.

But as she reached the last stair, the music stopped. She looked up. The firelight fell on the face of the dancer—Esmeralda's face.

"Ah," she called. "The dancing woman, with the dancing bear."

Gemma swallowed.

Esmeralda turned again, her skirts swirling. "Here's to hoping that you find your way back to being a fine lady."

Gemma hurried by. The bear eyed them as it clumped on, and Gemma thought of putting a hand to its head, but it did not turn to them. They vanished into an alleyway, and Gemma hurried along it.

She had reckoned the streets rightly. They came out next to Queen Shulamith's house. The first carriages had arrived, and the guests descending in glitter. A vendor in the street hawked delicate little butterflies, red, orange, or blue, for the fine ladies to wear in their hair.

Gemma let her breath out. It was well that Queen Shulamith wanted them to come not so early in the ball. She edged toward the doorway.

A carriage drew out, and Lady Maude swept out. Though arrayed with diamonds on blue, she looked as if she had bitten something sour. Gemma stopped. Moments later, a young woman with curly brown hair came out, and then, black-haired, in a yellow gown, Marjorie appeared. Perhaps she should have chosen a different rose bush; the color was not perfectly for her hair, but—

"At least she kept her word about letting her," Gemma murmured, and went inside. The obfuscation spell should work until she addressed the queen, and the arriving guests did indeed notice no more of either of them than a bit from the corner of their eyes. Marjorie thought she saw a flick of red, but though she knew Gemma would appear to entertain them, she could not be sure that it was the woman's skirt. She would have to wait to learn that the woman was well—and her bear, too.

In Lady Maude's wake, she swept up the stairs toward the doors. Lady Maude would certainly have no reason to complain of her behavior at the ball. Other guests clumped about the door. Her gaze passed over them, noting this one and that, and faltered on Luc. He looked up and at her, smiled, and kissed his hand to her.

Feeling her cheeks heat, she looked down. She hurried after Lady Maude and Henrietta, to the doors, which revealed a chamber glittering. Candlelight filled it and reflected from the mirror opposite. She drew a deep breath and reminded herself of her manners: before all else, they had to greet Queen Shulamith.

The queen wore a dark indigo gown, not adorned with so much as pleating, and no jewelry, but even with her dark hair spread over her shoulders like any maid's, it was impossible to mistake her for anyone else. They glided into the line of guests, and Marjorie eyed the room as they waited, inching forward now and again. The ball had certainly drawn out the peacocks in the city. Even at balls, she had never seen such extravagance before, not in dyes, or ribbons, or jewelry.

And the mirror that covered the wall opposite to them—was that one of the mirrors of Queen Shulamith? She had heard tales of them—an unusual number of tales, even in this city, for something that no one had seen. Her gaze went over the reflected ball-goers, and then it stopped. Held prisoner by the image of a young woman in a yellow gown, her blond hair falling free over her shoulders. With that color hair, the yellow gown became her. Better than Marjorie's own gown of the same hue.

She stood next to Lady Maude and Henrietta, too—that blond, reflected maid.

Marjorie's hand jerked up to take up a lock of her own hair. Black, still dyed black. But in the mirror, the image had taken up a lock of blond hair and looked at it. . . .

Lady Maude's whisper broke in: "*Marjorie.*"

Even with all the fury in that name, Marjorie barely managed to look up. Henrietta pouted, Lady Maude glanced between her and the mirror and slowly looked appalled, and Queen Shulamith laughed, deep in her throat.

"I see," said the queen, "that you have seen the first of my mirrors."
Then her gaze went past Marjorie, toward the door. Her eyebrows went
up.

Among the throngs, drawing many gazes, two wan young boys.
dressed in black, wriggled into the room—far too young to be up, let
alone to attend a ball. They sidled along the wall, their faces and hair
pale against their dark clothing, and when the taller saw that Queen
Shulamith looked at him, he froze like a frightened fawn.

Mischief, thought Marjorie. And then—perhaps not—as all about
her, ball-goers noted the boys, to shake their heads and whispered, she
looked at the mirror. It could show the truth, it seemed.

It showed something looming over the boys. Too tall to be human,
too pale, too *tenuous*—a ghost, thought Marjorie, with cruel clawed
hands.

Then she realized that some of the staring ball-goers were staring at
her. Lady Maude looked ready to strike her, Henrietta seemed about to
sink into the floor, and others—others turned toward the mirror and
paid Marjorie no more heed.

Shouts rose, of horror. Ball-goers, almost as pale as the reflection,
pressed away from the mirrors, even toward the boys. The boys looked
at the mirror and grew paler. The older one held the younger's hand
tightly. The pale monster grew taller, thicker—more substantial? Marjorie felt the air growing colder about them, and after a moment, she
blinked, trying to clear her vision. It did not help, nor did blinking
again. The air seemed to have steeped in some dark miasma that
dragged light into itself and swallowed it whole.

Silvio drew his sword.

Luc said, dryly, "That's not likely to work," but drew his own. All
the adventure they had claimed to long for, right here in the ball. He
strode forward, toward the boys; if only he could get between the boys
and that ghostly monster.

"That will not work, gallant sir." Queen Shulamith's deep voice rang through the room. "They must go in there."

She pointed to another door. The ghost loomed, its hands descending toward the boys, and they grew almost as pale as it. The taller tried to take a step, and staggered.

Luc put up his sword, faster than he had known he could, and ran toward them. Footsteps echoed behind him, and when he reached and started to pick up the taller boy, Silvio appeared beside him to snatch the smaller. Neither boy struggled. Luc made the mistake of glancing at the mirror. The ghost loomed over their head. Its mouth gaped wide enough to swallow all four of them, and even its barely formed face could show anger.

Luc ran.

The ball-goers gaped and stared and did not move from the way. Some even pressed closer; Luc brushed by one portly lady, colliding with her gown, and left her exclaiming on his rudeness as he ran on, into the other room.

Fewer people had entered here already. Candles gleamed, and another mirror stood the length of the wall.

A few strides in, Luc stopped. The boy leaned on his shoulder as if too weak to straighten, but the mirror showed no monster—not even when Silvio followed with the other boy. He dragged in a deep breath. Abruptly, the air warmed and seemed to clear, so that all things sparkled again.

Marjorie slowly walked toward them. In the doorway, she called, "Bring them back here." Then she glanced at Queen Shulamith, who nodded.

Luc silently obeyed, and looked into the mirror on that side. It showed no sign of the monster, yet.

Marjorie touched the boy's hair. "Good evening," she whispered. "Who are you?"

"Michel," whispered the boy, and the ball-goers turned away, talking with great to-do about the monsters and the mirror, and how this would swamp anything else about the ball, and what a pity that such festivities would be marred by such a freakish event. Marjorie stepped closer. The smaller boy began to whimper against Silvio's shoulder, and Silvio scowled, but Michel straightened to look at him. "Philippe—" He pointed.

"Where do you come from?"

"From Great-great-grandfather's—" Michel wriggled, and Luc put him down. Silvio put down Philippe, and Michel grabbed his hand before inching through their tale of their dead parents, and how Great-great-grandfather had charge of them in his white house, and how they had left.

And Marjorie, bent to listen, pieced together the bits. And when they said their parents' names—"But you are my cousins!"

Michel blinked.

"You are my father's mother's brother's daughter's sons! I heard of how my cousin died, but I did not think of her sons." She straightened. And she had been so distraught that it meant staying with Maude. "It is clear that your care does not suit so elderly a gentleman. In the morning I will come to visit him, and offer to take you from his hands."

The boys' eyes looked like saucers. She would manage, Marjorie told herself. However much Lady Maude was offended, somehow she would manage to get these boys away from whatever haunted house that elderly *wretch* had inflicted on them.

"For now," she said, "I will send you home with servants."

"There is no need, Lady Marjorie." Queen Shulamith had come up so silently that she blinked in surprise; the woman's full skirts spread like the night sky, and Marjorie blinked, thinking she saw stars in the folds.

The queen smiled benignly on them all. "I will send a candleman with them myself. I have no wish for any guest of mine, however young, to have trouble returning to his home." And she bent to take the children's hands. With great wondering gazes, they took them.

"How did it work?" said Luc.

"Why, gallant sir, this mirror *sees* the truth." She nodded to the mirror showing Marjorie's pale hair. "And the mirror that you went to, *shows* the truth."

Marjorie fingered her dyed locks. She wondered whether she should go into that room, ever. This mirror showed what things really looked like. That mirror showed only what was visible, and made what was invisible vanish—because it showed no monster, there was no monster to be shown. She bit her lip. Lady Maude would be glad to shove her into it, she had no doubts. It would show her with black hair, and then the spell would not need renewing.

Queen Shulamith's smile deepened. "There is always that door." She nodded across the room. "There, the mirror both sees, and shows, the truth."

Marjorie turned and hurried toward it. The thick press made it worse than carrying the boys to the other room. Her skirts brushed those of many another lady, and some garlands lay strewn in her path. Ladies murmured behind their fans about such hoydenish behavior, and Luc looked after her.

"Will everything be such an uproar?" demanded a portly man, middle-aged, dressed in crimson velvet. "What sort of ball has such confusion? Will it last the length of it?"

"There is no need for it to last," said Queen Shulamith. "The mirrors can reveal only what is hidden." She smiled. "How many secrets can one ball hold?"

Her gaze went to the door that Marjorie had taken, and drew other gazes with it. The boys, wide-eyed, looked from her to the door and back. The murmurs did not perturb either her calm smile, or her steady gaze, until Marjorie reappeared.

She stood in the doorway and smiled radiantly. Her hair spread, golden, over her shoulders.

Lady Maude looked as if she had eaten a far too sour pickle, and Queen Shulamith stepped closer to her to murmur, "Certainly the gown is more pleasing with the true color. Why, she all but glows like the sun."

Lady Maude glared at her, but said nothing. About the ballroom, women edged toward the other room; some had fair hair, but most were dark. Marjorie herself walked across the room toward Lady Maude, and Luc slipped closer to her.

Gemma appeared in a doorway—not one of those with a mirror. She looked about until her gaze settled on Queen Shulamith, and the queen looked back. Then she curtsied, very deeply.

More deeply than to any other royalty or nobility in the city, thought Silvio.

Queen Shulamith turned, her dark skirt flowing out like the petals of a flower. "Listen," she called. "Come to see the dancing done by a bear and a woman."

"Come see how it's done," called Silvio. "Or the ladies will complain that you can not dance as well as a bear."

Laughter resounded. Queen Shulamith stepped aside with the boys. Luc closed the distance quickly, to offer Marjorie his arm. She smiled and took it. He felt almost light-headed—she looked so much more lovely with her hair its true shade—and they joined the throngs. The music struck up, and the ball-goers formed measures, and in their midst, Gemma danced with the bear, with a crowd gathered around her.

A shrill, imperious voice rang over all. "There she is!"

Guards appeared in the doorway, and in their center stood Reinette, flushed with anger and in an unbecoming violet gown. She glared at Gemma and the bear as if the room held no one else.

"Arrest her!" Her hoarse voice resounded. Her arm went up and pointed at the dancer.

The guards glanced about.

"Arrest her?" said Queen Shulamith, mildly. "At my ball?"

"You false queen!" raged Reinette. "You pretender!"

Marjorie's lips curved without her thinking of it. All about her muffled laughter showed that others also thought what havoc it would wreak on the city, to punish all who claimed false titles.

"And you shelter an impostor!" Reinette drew a deep breath, and her lip curled. "A wayfaring entertainer, indeed. That woman is a sorceress and a servant of Queen Lenore!" Reinette lowered her voice. "She can mean you no good. She can mean none of you any good at all."

"Oh, that tale," said a man with disgust.

"That *true* tale," said Reinette. "She was unspeakably insolent to me today. And a wizard revealed to me the truth. She would not have dared if she were not Queen Lenore's *pet*." She pointed, and her soldiers stared to move.

"What means this invasion?" called Marjorie. "Bringing armed forces within the city?"

"You are part and party to this treachery," said Reinette. "Sheltering that woman in your plot! Why else would any noble, let alone royal, have a care for a mere street entertainer?" She looked about. "There is a plot!"

The bear sat back on its haunches. "Yes, there is."

Silence rippled out, and faces went pale. Reinette took a step backward.

"But it is not Mistress Gemma's, pretender, false queen."

"You fool," whispered Gemma, her face paling—and the room so quiet that most of them heard her. "The danger."

The bear did not take its gaze from Reinette. "Where in all the laws does it decree that a bear, being the son of the king and queen, *can not* ascend the throne?"

"She has soldiers with her," said Gemma, despairing.

Reinette, her mouth set in mulish lines, took a step forward with her guards.

Silvio drew his sword; the sound rang in the room. Moments later, Luc did as well, Marjorie stepping away without a moment's thought, and other gentlemen—most young, some older, some completely old—and the ladies drew back, whispering among themselves, to leave the space clear. Gemma swallowed. To fight already. . . .

"Sir Bear," said Queen Shulamith, "what brings you to my humble ball?"

The bear bowed—as gracefully as it danced. "Your Majesty. I sought out the mirrors of your fame." It started to lumber off, and Gemma hurried beside it. The ladies, murmuring, parted only enough to let the two of them through. Marjorie felt her heart hammer, and glanced at her hair—still wheat-golden on her shoulders. Then she sidled toward the door. She did not reach it before a murmur spread outward. When she reached the doorway, a man, wrapped in a bearskin, knelt on the floor. A handsome young man. Her breath gushed out.

"Whatever does this mean?" whispered Henrietta.

"Why," said Marjorie dryly, pitching her voice to carry, "don't you notice how much he resembles Reinette? His cousin Reinette? He's the rightful king, the one who was born a bear."

Gemma, still very pale, said, "Queen Lenore's first born and second son were murdered by poison. She thought being born a bear would protect the child." She spread her hands. "She was right."

"You're an impostor," snarled Reinette, stalking through the crowd. With the guards to either hand, the crowd pulled back, and none of the gentlemen seemed ready to strike the first blow. Though they pulled closer to where the prince stood. Most of the dancers pulled farther away.

Gemma looked trapped. Marjorie sidled along the wall. For a moment, she glimpsed Maud turning red with rage, but she walked on until she came to the opposite side. There, she stepped out to take Gemma's hands and pull her back, toward the garden doors.

"Stay out of the way," she said in a low voice. "They will be able to fight more freely if the swords come into play." Then she realized how still the ballroom was, and how her voice carried. Reinette looked banefully at her.

"I don't want them to fight," said Gemma, with intensity. "The prince does not even have a sword—"

Silvio, with a flourish, drew off his mantle and offered to the prince. "You have the swords of loyal men, Your Highness."

"There is," said the prince, his voice still half growling, "no need for us to taint Queen Shulamith's ball. I shall withdraw and return to my native land to claim—"

"I will not have it!" shouted Reinette, raising her hands. Her guards looked at her, weighed their dangers, and drew their swords.

"Into the gardens, my men," said the prince. "I do not have so many of you that I can risk your lives."

Gemma grabbed Marjorie's hand. "Us first," she whispered. Marjorie scrambled with her out the doors.

The night was cool, and dew already formed on the grass. The ballroom's windows cast great golden squares of light across the lawn—making the shadows between them still darker, and hard to penetrate.

"The rose garden," said Marjorie.

"That will be a labyrinth," said Gemma.

Marjorie, remembering the invasion, said, "Exactly." Then she hurried toward the flowery scent. She glanced back. Gemma followed her, and then the prince, and his men.

The center, she told herself, as she walked between the first two hedges. From there, no doubt, they could escape to the city's labyrinthine streets—who would build a labyrinth without such magic?—and get inside some building where Reinette could not easily follow.

She turned right. That was usually the first turn, no one wished his guests to be baffled and angry by the time they solved the maze. Her confidence carried; the prince and the gentlemen followed her, down this turn and that one and around and about.

The maze turned and branched and towered over her until Marjorie felt quite certain that she would have to confess to having gotten them all lost—and instantly a square appeared before them, the grass dew-laden but even, and rising toward a hillock. Marjorie ran toward it before she remembered that she had seen no hillock from the windows—and after as well. However this hillock appeared here, even if it had done so when they hurried through the maze, she had to see.

Such as she could. More shadows than light fell over the garden. Here and there, lamplight glanced from swords or armor, but most of the movement was dim and hard to make out. She swallowed. First of all, to find a way out. . . .

"You are watching your plan from here?" said the prince, his voice deep, as he came to stand beside her.

"My plan—but my hope, first," said Marjorie.

The prince glanced at her—she could the light glint from his eye—but Gemma gasped, and pointed.

"That hedge," she said. "It moved."

The men gathered about them and watched the labyrinth in silence, as the walls rose, and shifted, and the guards caught in them bellowed in rage and tried to turn their swords in axes. Roses shifted about them.

Marjorie turned her face away. She did not want to see the roses turn on the men.

Silvio called, "Look!" He pointed, with his left hand. A handful of guards staggered from the maze onto the grass. The gentlemen all braced themselves.

"I am the prince," the prince called. "The rightful prince. You all know how the queen's children died, one by one, until finally she gave birth to a bear—to shelter her last child from his enemies."

Silence fell. No one moved.

"Are you among those enemies?"

The guards bowed their heads, and turned to offer him the hilts of their swords. Gemma let her breath out slowly.

"This," she murmured, "has been a ramshackle and disorderly night. Hardly a ball at all."

The prince glanced sideways at her, and for a moment, she thought he looked fond.

"When was it not, my lady? From the hour when we left my mother's house, when were we not desperately pondering another way to take even the next step?"

Gemma let her breath out, slowly.

Marjorie whispered, "There ought to be a way out."

Gemma nodded, and looked down at the hedges. Then she blinked. "When did that happen?"

They all turned, one by one, as the first one stared and could not look away.

Queen Shulamith smiled benevolently upon them. Gemma wondered how much of the light could fall on her without seeming to shift through the air. The hedges, she knew, could move, but now they had moved to stand at either hand of the queen, leaving a wide and stately path.

"I would be a negligent hostess to let you scramble off now," she said. She inclined her head. "If you truly wish to leave, you may do so with dignity and grace."

The prince bowed, awkwardly. "Your Majesty, I fear I am not attired for a ball."

Her smile broadened. "Come within, come within—my Lady Marjorie, could you assist Lady Gemma within?"

Gemma remembered starting to descend, but did not quite follow all the rest until finally she stood among the ball-goers in her poppy-scarlet gown—a flower among the flowers of this field, no different from another—except that she could see the others gazing on her with more poison that she had ever seen in her life.

Some, she had to grant, were merely curious.

But one, aglitter with diamonds, descended on the two of them. Gemma frowned, thinking she should know her, but her face was so contorted with rage that she could not be recognized. At least on brief acquaintance—Marjorie stood still with recognition.

The woman surged close enough to whisper, "You little fool." She glared at Marjorie. "What were you *thinking*?"

Marjorie lifted her eyebrows, but Gemma thought she could see the strain. "Why, preventing discord at a ball. It's very unsuitable. A ball should have harmony. It was only courteous to our hostess the queen."

Lady Maud clapped her hand on Marjorie's arm. "You will have a chance to reconsider that in your chamber—"

"Her Majesty asked me to stay with Lady Gemma," said Marjorie.

"Lady Gemma?" Maud's lip curled.

"The prince said so," said Marjorie. "And you know that he is only not king because he is not crowned. Yet. The authority was his from the hour that his father died."

"When he pranced about the street for coins as a bear?"

"Yes," said Silvio, by her elbow. Maud turned her vicious expression on him, and he wondered whether she intended to make a spectacle of herself. But he had his commission from his king. He bowed to Gemma. "My lady, a new dance comes. Will you do me the honor of becoming my partner?"

Gemma hesitated. He had asked her once before, and not been a worse dancer than a bear. Perhaps she could even ask him what he had suspected, then. She nodded, and glanced at Marjorie, and saw Luc advancing to claim her hand, and Maud, sourly, withdrawing.

Was it not half the purpose of a ball to marry off the maidens? thought Gemma, feeling almost light-headed. She should be glad of a proper match for Marjorie, and with a man that the king would favor.

Music started, and the dance began. Silvio did not take her to the center of the floor, where all eyes would be on them, and she felt glad of it, though it was not so hard to remember, how to dance with a man instead of a bear. It had been easier in the stairway, out of sight.

"You dance even more gracefully than before," said Silvio.

"Perhaps your thoughts are less on your suspicions," said Gemma.

He sighed. "I must confess that my suspicions were too slight to claim any credit."

As the last measures ended, she found herself on the edge of the figure, and when she started to turn, the prince stood there and looked at her, smiling. Dressed better than most of the dancers—she would have been astounded to see such green velvet watching them on the street, and then expected gold from him.

Silvio bowed, and she remembered her curtsy. Then the prince bowed to her to ask the honor of the dance.

"I hope that I will master it in human form as well as in bear," said the prince.

"Will that be so difficult?" said Gemma.

He spread his hands. "You remember how I needed a servant to page through a book when I read it—my paws could not be trusted to turn it. There seems to be an art that I must master."

She curtsied again. "It would be my pleasure to aid you in mastery."

Silvio edged off, thinking he half-felt pleased that the prince did not act in love with her, even though the prince had to make a good alliance with his marriage, under any circumstances. He looked about for Luc and Marjorie, ready to claim Marjorie as a partner where Luc had to let her go.

The next dance was slow and stately, and most of the dancers left the floor, to stand where they could see the prince.

"You do not seem eager to gawk," said Marjorie.

"His Highness," said Silvio, "asked us to attend him when he returns to his kingdom."

"You—and Luc?"

Silvio nodded.

After a moment, Marjorie said, "I wish I could remain all hours and claim dances with you twain, but—I must rise earlier tomorrow."

Silvio's eyebrows went up.

"And do you know where the prince is staying? I doubt it will being whatever corner he and she were sleeping while they feigned they were common street-entertainers."

"Her Majesty offered to let them remain the night."

Marjorie nodded. When the dance ended, she took another partner and danced every dance, even once with the prince, before the clock struck midnight, when she went to bid Queen Shulamith farewell.

Queen Shulamith smiled upon her, and told her that a candleman awaited her at the door. "To get you safely home."

Marjorie thanked her and, her heart hammering, evaded both Maud and Henrietta on the way out. The candleman by the door muttered a little under his breath, and his nose was ruddy, but the candles on his hat were all brightly lit, and he led the way off steadily. Marjorie swallowed again and wondered how Queen Shulamith had known in advance that she would not leave in Maud's carriage—but she had spoken of leaving early, and rumors always spread at balls.

The lights of Queen Shulamith's ball receded behind them, and the moon shone down on them and reflected off the river when they reached it. Moths descended in silvery streams, but the enchantment on the candlelight kept even them a ways off.

The candleman began to carol an improbable ballad about a madman whom the moon had fallen in love with, and shortly thereafter, showed her to the door. The maid at the door looked startled. Then, she had to wonder at the hair, with all the fuss about the dye.

After a minute, the maid croaked, "Lady Maud?"

Marjorie blinked. Oh, yes, she had come alone and without the carriage, too.

"Is well and enjoying the ball. I returned alone rather disturb her." Marjorie glanced at the dark and silent rooms. Only a candle by the door gave any light. "The other servants ran off to a servants' ball, and left you here to let them in again?"

The maid flushed. She knew, thought Marjorie, who would be blamed.

"I won't tell Lady Maud," Marjorie said, lit her candle off the maid's, and headed up the stairs. The yellow gown came off easily, as if true cloth. She wondered how long the gown would last. . . a lavish gift, if it lasted like cloth.

The moonlight cast its light on the floor in lopsided squares, with a few moths having found their way to the glass. She snuffed the candle and went to the window before she went to bed. From it, she could still see the lights at Queen Shulamith's ball, all golden. Moths launched themselves from the now dark window. Some wavered through the air as far as the ball itself, where the dancing went on and on.

Before the sky was even gray, the first workers trudged out on the street and passed by it, and bore the news the rest of their way, that the dancers at Queen Shulamith's ball would be going to bed at dawn—

"If that," said one pastry vendor, as she handed out lukewarm meat pastries to carpenters and seamstresses plodding off to work.

"All the more work for the shoemakers," said one gray-haired seamstress, dourly, and carried the news onward. She found the servants leaving their ball, and assured them that even now they could dance the hours away without their masters' catching their mischief.

"They'll expect work to be done," said Lady Maud's cook, and with the rest, they headed back to their houses as the sky turned charcoal gray, and then paler shades. It was when they closed the door that Marjorie awoke. She looked out the window and saw it was still dove gray, with tinges of pink and yellow, and then she remembered that she had left the ball early because she needed to rise early. And why. She might have to call on the prince's favor.

Up and dressed in a respectable gray gown, she descended the stairs in search of breakfast, and servants scrambled as if caught by a sorceress. Marjorie's eyebrows went up, but she merely silently took her breakfast. And told the maid that they had to go for a walk.

The maid was silently behind her until she reached the pale house she intended. She breathed out sharply. "You can't—"

Marjorie was through the gate, passing among the statues, and up the stairs before the maid could bring herself to object. She rapped with the knocker and waited. The maid still stood by the gate. Perhaps she did not fear dismissal so much now, when Marjorie already knew how the servants had gone runagate while Queen Shulamith's ball had gone on.

The door creaked open. Michel looked up at her. Philippe half hid behind him. They still wore mourning, and still looked pale against it, but even now, she thought they had more roses in their cheeks.

"I give you good morning," she said. "I have come to see your great-great-grandfather."

"He's not here," blurted out Philippe.

"Not anywhere," said Michel, his fingers tightening on the door-knob. "We've looked. And no servants, either."

Marjorie looked between them. "That will make my case all the easier, but I will have to look myself." She stepped inside and glanced back at the gate. The maid shuddered and wrapped her shawl more closely about herself. Marjorie's eyes rolled, but she set out with the boys, upstairs and down, looking in scores of room, mostly empty, scaring up occasional cobwebs and dust, but no sign of any other human habitation, until finally they came out the backdoor, into the garden

Philippe squealed. "Look at the fishes!"

The boys scrambled over. At a more sedate pace—she had not only danced many dances, they had scrambled far, searching the house—Marjorie came over. Great enormous goldfish swam with the murky pool. Some pale with brilliantly red-gold splotches like coins, some gold as pure as a king's crown, some fiery red all over, like the sunset. The boys started to gabble something about how they had been paler, before.

"How striking," said Marjorie. "But I think it more important to deal with you." She inclined her head, and the boys looked up. "I thought to offer to take your guardianship, which is perhaps too great a burden for his years, since I am your cousin. With his having vanished like that—"

She hesitated. The boys' pale faces were utterly innocent. Perhaps later she would tell them. Now— "Come with me, then, and we will have the prince let me take it."

"Oh, can he?" said Michel.

He had better, thought Marjorie, after last night. Now, she only forced a smile and offered her hands. The boys hesitated before taking one apiece, and letting her lead them out to the street—around the house. Marvelous though Queen Shulamith's mirrors were, she did not quite trust them to unhaunt a house.

The maid blinked, but fell in behind her and the boys as they walked down the streets toward Queen Shulamith's house. Here and there, stores pulled open the doors to their wares, and Marjorie tugged the boys from the more fascinating ones. They met vendors on the way, and working folks bustling to their jobs, and even a few merchants, or housewives venturing to the stores, but only at the street itself did she see nobility as they sleepily stumbled down the stairs. She glanced sideways down the street. The coachmen looked a little more awake; she hoped they had had a chance to rest before they collided all the way down the streets.

But she could do nothing about that. She headed up the stairs as others headed down, and garnered many stares. Her gray gown stuck out among all the finery, however much the dancing had left that bedraggled, and eyebrows went up as those departing picked out the boys in their black, and yet—she set her jaw—she headed for the great doors as if there were no others.

The prince emerged, with Luc and Silvio behind him, and Gemma on his arm. She angled over.

He stopped at the sight of her. She freed her hands to curtsy, and the boys gawked for a moment and then bowed.

"I came to petition, Your Highness. These boys my cousins are the wards of their great-great-grandfather. Whose age, I dare say, made him unfit for the role, even if his family feeling made him take it on. You saw how they arrived last night—" Her words choked off, remembering the ghostly figures. She swallowed. The prince still studied her in silence. "I went to offer myself as a more hale guardian. And I found that his house had neither him, nor any of his servants—only the boys. So I brought them to petition you for their guardianship. And to take charge of the house, as part of their inheritance, if he can not be found."

No one asked why she thought the boys had inherited. They had guessed what the figures meant.

The prince smiled—and then yawned. He spoke with care. "I am glad that you have not asked for something requiring deep thought. Certainly, who could be more fit?"

Marjorie let her breath out. She still had to deal with Maud, but with the guardianship in hand, she had an argument that her aunt could not ignore.

The prince went on without pause. "And—" He glanced sideways. "I must return to my kingdom. It is not fitting that Lady Gemma should travel without a companion of noble birth."

"How true," said Marjorie. And with her hair blond again, Maud would probably be glad to see the back of her.

"There is much to be done," said the prince, meditatively. "I must start here—find a place to stay—"

"You can lease the house," said Michel, chirpily. They all looked at him. "It's all *different* now, not haunted."

"And you will charge the rent?"

Michel looked at his shoes.

Gemma cleared her throat. "We have gold enough. I saved the coins so that everyone would take us for street entertainers indeed. It would pay several months lease on even a fine home."

The prince's eyebrows went up. "You seemed to have arranged everything well."

Queen Shulamith appeared in the doorway. "Good morning," she said. "Come within, and all may be justly discussed."

Two little schoolgirls, on the way to Queen Hesione's school, watched them go in.

"They're going to add that to our lessons," said one gloomily. "The prince who was a bear and how the queen had protected him."

"We don't get to go to the ball," said the other, "but we have to *study* it."

They hurried on. From a high up window, a handful of gossips looked down from their narrow window.

"Really, this will encourage them like nothing else," said Alixandre. "Turning back into a prince and claiming the throne?"

"And," said Ida, "turning that lass into a fine lady."

Blanca lifted her cup. "Perhaps a few ladies should try fortune-telling, or dancing with bears, if they wish to mend their fortunes."

Alixandre shrugged. "So the tales have always told." She drank her tea.

Also by Mary Catelli

Curses And Wonders
Dragon Slayer
Eyes of the Sorceress
Fever and Snow
Mermaids' Song
Sword and Shadow
The Book of Bone
Witch-Prince Ways
Dragonfire and Time
Enchantments And Dragons
Jewel of the Tiger
Over the Sea, To Me
The Dragon's Cottage
The Maze, the Manor, and the Unicorn
The White Menagerie
A Diabolical Bargain
Madeleine and the Mists
Magic And Secrets
The Lion and the Library
The Princess Goes Into The Forest
The Wolf and the Ward
The Witch-Child and the Scarlet Fleet
Treachery And Spells
Winter's Curse
Crow Curse

Free Passage
Isabelle and the Siren
Journeys And Wizardry
Lifestone
Magic of the Lost God
Never Comment On A Likeness
One Name
The Drunken Mermaids
The Turtle in the Sea of Sand
Were I You
Where There Is Smoke
Through A Mirror, Darkly
The Princess Seeks Her Fortune
Queen Shulamith's Ball

About the Author

Mary Catelli is an avid reader of fantasy, science fiction, history, fairy tales, philosophy, folklore and a lot of other things. (Including the backs of cereal boxes.) Which, in due course, overflowed into writing fantasy (and some science fiction).